SWEET SURRENDER

ELITE HEIRS OF MANHATTAN BOOK 2

MISSY WALKER

To Jo, It's not going to be the same without you x

Elite *Men* Of Manhattan and
Elite *Heirs* of Manhattan Family Tree

BARRETT BLACK
LOURDE DIAMOND

FORBIDDEN LUST #1
FORBIDDEN LOVE #2

CONNOR DIAMOND
PEPPER LITTLE

LOST LOVE #3

ARI GOLDSMITH
OLIVIA WILLOWS

MISSING LOVE #4

MAGNUS MILLER
EVELYN BLACK

GUARDED LOVE #5

COLTON
BLACK

SIENNA
BLACK

LUCIAN
DIAMOND

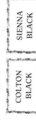

ROSE
GOLDSMITH

NOAH
GOLDSMITH

ARIA
MILLER

VALENTINA
MILLER

MILES
YOUNG

SEDUCTIVE HEARTS #1
COLTON AND ROSE

SWEET SURRENDER #2
NOAH AND SIENNA

1

SIENNA
TEN YEARS AGO

Was it possible to die of nervousness?

My hands were shaking so hard I had to consciously tell myself to calm down before I ran them over the front of the ice-blue dress I had secretly bought and smuggled into the penthouse while the rest of the family was out.

I was a princess, right down to the full skirt and the intricate arrangement of curls pinned against the back of my head.

Everybody was going to lose their shit when I walked into the winter formal on Pierce Jameson's arm. Nobody knew he had invited me. I hadn't even told my best friend, Rose, and we told each other everything. But this was different. I didn't feel like hearing Pierce was too old for me. Not only that, but I also didn't want her to tell her brother Noah, who was best friends with my brother, Colton. I knew Noah wouldn't be able to help himself. He would inevitably tell Colton, and I knew neither of them would want me hanging around them and the other upperclassmen like I would ruin their good time or something. And I probably would because I knew the sort of stuff they liked to do. They wouldn't want to drink in front of me in case I tattled on them or whatever.

I didn't care about any of that, though I knew they wouldn't believe me. I only wanted to be with Pierce. Ever since we first started talking on Snapchat, it was like life had color. There was something to be excited about when I first woke up and something to smile about as I fell asleep at night—having a secret with somebody like Pierce, somebody I'd had a crush on ever since I first saw him during freshman orientation. He was so tall with thick, golden hair and the kind of smile that made me forget how to breathe.

And he wanted *me*.

"We have to be careful around everybody else. Your brother would be pissed if he knew we were talking." He was right, which was why I always pretended we didn't know each other when we'd passed in the halls at school.

Pierce being three years older meant we didn't see much of each other, which made it easy. I could keep my eyes looking straight ahead instead of staring at him, offering a secret smile, looking for a sign that he remembered everything we shared when it was just the two of us messaging on the phone.

I smoothed a strand of chocolate brown hair behind my ear before reapplying my pink lip gloss. There was fear in my blue eyes when I met my reflection in the mirror over my dresser. Colton would probably be pissed when he saw me with a senior, somebody in his class. I was taking a risk, hoping he wouldn't do something stupid like demand I go home or maybe cause a scene or whatever. For once, I needed him to behave himself and not act like a complete dick. Maybe if he saw how happy I was, he would leave me alone. We could deal with everything in the morning.

Mom and Dad were out at some dinner, and Colton had planned on getting ready at Noah's, meaning there was nobody in the penthouse to think anything of me walking around in a ball gown. The heels of my silver shoes tapped the hardwood floors as I hurried around, checking my clutch to make sure I had everything I needed.

This would be fine.

Everything would be fine.

I was going to the winter formal with the boy of my dreams, whom I had spent weeks getting to know through dozens of conversations. Nothing would change once we were face-to-face. He would still be the same person—sweet, smart, and funny.

He knew so many things about me, the sort of stuff I never planned on telling anybody. When I was talking to him, it felt natural to share little parts of myself. I wanted him to know me as much as I wanted to know him.

From the bottom of my heart, I knew he would kiss me by the end of the night. My heart threatened to explode every time I thought about it. I only hoped it didn't literally explode when he did—when he took my face in his hands, pressed his lips against mine, and made all my dreams come true.

"*I promise I'll be a gentleman, though I can't promise I won't want a kiss.*" He had even said that to make sure I didn't freak out. The memory made my skin tingle and warmed my face even days after he'd first sent that particular message. My heart fluttered whenever I imagined closing my eyes and letting him touch his lips to mine, and I had imagined it a lot.

He was supposed to pick me up at seven. I checked my phone and blew out a huge, nervous breath.

Only a few more minutes.

Did I put on deodorant? Oh, God, this was either going to be amazing or a complete disaster if I didn't get my shit together. It wasn't the first dance I had ever been to, of course, but it was the first time things had ever been like this. I would be the youngest person there, for sure, and I would walk in with the hottest, most popular guy in the whole school.

Was it possible to peak at fifteen? I couldn't imagine life getting any better. "You've got this," I whispered to myself in the mirror near the front door. "He likes you. He wouldn't have asked you if he didn't."

And for all I knew, we would be telling this story one day. Maybe during our wedding anniversary—a big party for our twenty-fifth—we would describe how we'd connected secretly behind everybody's backs and how we announced our relationship to the whole world at the winter formal.

All of that flew out the window when there was a knock at the door. I almost dropped my purse but managed to keep hold of it at the last second, taking a few deep breaths before squaring my shoulders and opening the door.

This was it.

This was when the rest of my life started.

Which was what made the sight of Noah Goldsmith so confusing. He was alone, dressed in a tux, and smirking as he looked me up and down. I was fully dressed but had never felt so exposed.

"What are you doing here?" I demanded. If it hadn't been for his smirk, I might have been worried something happened to Colton. "Shouldn't you be at the dance by now?"

Instead of answering, he let out a high-pitched whistle. "You look nice. What are you so dressed up for?"

"Don't worry about it." I hated the way my voice shook. He wasn't supposed to find out this way, not until we got to the dance. "So, really, why are you here? I thought you guys were getting ready for the formal at your parents' place."

"Yeah, everybody's on their way to the hotel. I wanted to swing by and see you before I joined them." Folding his arms, his expression hardened into the same look I had seen so many times before from him, my brother, and their friends. Arrogant. Cocky. His chestnut brown hair gleamed in the light above the front door when he tipped his head to the side. "If I didn't know better, I would think you were dressed up for the formal too. But that can't be possible since you're only a freshman. So where are you going tonight?"

"Maybe I *am* going to the formal." Because fuck him and his attitude. I lifted my chin and smiled. "I'm going with Pierce Jameson. Now you know. You were going to find out soon, anyway."

I figured his mouth would fall open and his dark eyes bulge. I'd already envisioned the whole thing so many times. But never had I imagined him snorting with laughter before asking, "Are you sure about that?"

"Well... yeah?" I replied with a laugh of my own. "He asked me, and I said yes."

"Why would he do that?"

This was going terribly. He was going to ruin everything if Pierce showed up while he was still standing in the doorway, acting like a dick. My pulse picked up speed at the thought. "Why is it any of your business?" I countered. "Go, have fun. I'll see you there in a little while."

"I hate to tell you, but you'll be waiting a while." He blurted out a laugh, shaking his head. "Really, my bad. I shouldn't have let it go this far. It looks like you, like... went all-out with the dress and hair. But maybe now you've learned your lesson."

"I don't understand."

Rolling his eyes, he groaned, "Pierce isn't coming to pick you up. He's already there with Penny Schwartz." When he laughed again, all I could do was stare at him and wait for him to tell me he was kidding. "Come on, Sienna. Did you seriously think he was into you? He's a fucking senior. Early admission to Harvard. Like he would screw around with a little girl like you."

Bile rushed into my throat once his words sank into my overloaded brain, and I started trembling as the pain set in. I couldn't believe it. I didn't want to. He was going to take it back any second.

Only he didn't. He looked as serious as I'd ever seen him, and I had known him my entire life.

Do not cry.

Do not.

"What are you saying?" I whispered, hoping he was kidding because the alternative was unthinkable.

Throwing his hands into the air, he nearly shouted, "I'm saying it was me, dumbass! Jesus Christ, you're slow on the uptake when you want to be. That's not even his Snapchat account I was messaging you from. Now, you know better than to mess around with the big boys."

"That's not true." I was shaking all over and barely fighting back tears. It was unbelievable. It couldn't be true. Weeks of talking, joking, getting to know each other. No way could Noah have fooled me like that. I knew him too well.

He arched an eyebrow. "I promise I'll be a gentleman, but I can't promise I won't want a kiss."

That was it. The proof I didn't actually need because deep down, I believed him. Standing in the foyer, dressed up nicer than I had ever been in my whole life, I knew it had all been a fantasy. How could I have been so stupid?

I wanted to die. I wanted to fold up in place and die right here on the floor. Anything would be better than standing there and listening to his laughter. Knowing he made a fool out of me. "Who knows about this?" I asked.

"I don't know." He waved a hand like it didn't mean anything. "We had a couple shots when we were getting ready, and I think I said something to Evan, maybe."

Evan? The whole damn school would know about it by the end of the weekend. My brother would find out. He'd probably tell our parents. I wouldn't be able to escape the humiliation no matter where I went. "How could you do this?" My voice was weak, small, and breathless.

"Like I said. You were the one staring at him during freshman orientation, so don't pretend you weren't. I saw you sitting in the auditorium, practically drooling while he gave his student council speech." There was so much contempt in his voice. It was like he hated me. "And as soon as you thought you were talking to him on Snapchat, you got all flirty and shit. It was pretty easy to make you believe you were talking to him."

"But how..." A sob sliced through me. I couldn't hide it, no matter how I knew I should. "How? Why would you do that to me?"

"Oh, come on. You learned a lesson. You didn't get hurt."

We both looked down at my clutch when my phone buzzed. I pulled it out without thinking, and at first, my hand shook hard enough that I couldn't read the message. Once I did, though, my stomach dropped further than it already had.

Unknown: *This is Penelope Schwartz. Just talked to Evan. Stay away from my man, bitch, or I'll kick your ass.*

I didn't realize Noah had leaned down to read the message until he grunted. "That girl has claws. She would tear you a new one. Like I said, you learned a lesson."

The know-it-all way he said it was what finally broke me. "Fuck *you*." I snarled before pressing both hands to his chest and shoving hard enough to make him stumble backward. "I didn't ask you to teach me anything. You did this because you're mean and nasty, and only a loser with an ugly soul could spend weeks making me... making me think..."

He ignored the tears filling my eyes and how I fought for every breath. "You're young. You'll get over it." He made a big deal of checking his watch while I gasped for air. "I better go. Everybody's waiting for me."

"Let me tell you one thing, Noah Goldsmith." There was a part of me he hadn't hurt—something hard and cold, sharp and deadly. And that part turned to stone as I glared up at him. "I'll be civil in front of our families, but otherwise... I wouldn't piss on you if you were on fire."

I had the satisfaction of watching his face fall before I slammed the door and locked it. In the nick of time, too, since my legs couldn't hold me up anymore.

My dress puffed up around me like a cloud as I sank to the floor, surrounded by satin and tulle and the shattered pieces of my heart.

2

NOAH

PRESENT DAY

"**Y**ou, my friend, are thoroughly fucked." Colton always did have a way with words.

"Thanks for your help. I knew it was the right move, meeting up with you tonight."

"Listen. I'm right there with you, wanting to know who the fuck made up this story. Once we find them, I'll gladly hold them still while you break every bone in their face." He set his drink down on the polished surface of the bar before lifting a shoulder. "But I mean, let's be honest, a bunch of gossip isn't going to do any permanent damage."

There were times when I wondered what the hell went on in his head. I had just finished telling him everything—losing my second listing in two weeks and the article due for syndication across the country in the morning. All the lies would hit the public in a matter of hours. Accusations which generally added up to me being the world's biggest piece of shit.

And there was nothing for me to do to stop it. I could only sit back and let some bullshit, fabricated article dictate my public image. I was on the verge of possibly losing everything I had worked my ass off for since college. That was when I first became interested in real estate investment. Everyone had expected me to follow in my dad's footsteps and eventually step up as CEO of Farrah Goldsmith Couture.

I knew what outsiders didn't. As far as Dad was concerned, it was Rose who would follow in his footsteps and fill his role once he stepped down. In his mind, it had always been Rose—serious and driven, practically a genius, so smart she'd skipped a grade in high school.

While all I'd ever been was mediocre, at least in his eyes. It wasn't like he'd built anything huge in his life—he took over his grandmother's company. Anybody could do that. His big contribution was making sure it didn't get run into the ground. Plenty of nepo babies specialized in doing that, strolling in and mismanaging everything until there was nothing left. The only difference here was Dad had only grown the company and ushered in its most prolific and profitable era. That much I could give him credit for, though I wasn't exactly breaking my back to do it.

Building something from scratch, on the other hand? That was my speed. I had managed to pull it off too. I'd built a luxury real estate empire on track to reach a billion-dollar valuation within the next two years.

Until this.

Until I'd gotten word of a hit piece due to go live tomorrow. I'd be accused of treating my client list like a dating pool. Undercutting rivals by fucking women, we were both courting professionally, luring them with my cock.

While my cock was known to work magic, I had never put it to work that way.

"It's easy for you to say this won't make a difference." I drained my glass and slammed it onto the bar, lifting my hand to catch the attention of the girl standing behind it. She offered a suggestive little smile before grabbing a bottle of Johnny Walker Blue from the top shelf and pouring me another.

"There you go," Colton murmured once she turned away to deal with somebody else. "She could help take your mind off things tonight. She's practically slobbering for you."

I need way more than an amateur fuck, not that Colton would understand.

"I could find willing pussy at every corner of this place," I reminded him. This was my third drink, and it still hadn't gone anywhere near releasing the tension that had plagued me all day. "Besides, I doubt she could take my mind off things."

He folded his arms on the bar and leaned a little closer, lowering his voice instead of raising it to be heard over the happy hour chatter around us. "Listen. I know everything seems pretty fucking grim at the moment, but you know how it is. Everybody's going to forget about it. Somebody's shithead kid is going to get in trouble, or some actress or singer will have a sex tape leaked, and that'll be it. Nobody will give a shit about you anymore."

Wouldn't it be nice if that were true? I wanted it to be, but I'd stopped believing in Santa years ago. "I don't think it's that simple. Somebody has a problem with me, and this is how they're handling it... planting some bullshit story about my company and what a shitty businessman I am. People don't forget shit like that. All it takes is a rumor to tank years of breaking my ass."

"You have one thing going for you. Sienna is the best at what she does. She'll fix everything."

He didn't notice the way I shifted in my chair. All of a sudden, there was a distinct pain in my ass. "You know how it is. She wouldn't piss on me if I were on fire." Her words were still as fresh and sharp as they were ten years ago.

"Oh, come on. You know Sienna." Colton wore the fond smirk of an older brother. "She's all bark, no bite. You don't have to be best friends to work together. We both know that."

He made a point. But it was one thing not to be friends and another to actively hate someone. Sienna had spent almost half her life loathing me for a stupid prank I'd played in my senior year. I would've bet anything she didn't remember the name of the guy she thought was taking her to that dance, but it didn't matter. She had decided she hated me, and that was how it would be.

Until then, I hadn't thought much about it. She was hardly the first person I had ever pissed off, and I was accustomed to ignoring shit like that. I had to be. How else could I get through life otherwise? I wouldn't be able to function.

Now, my professional reputation and my entire business and employees were in her hands.

"Didn't she recently handle that comedian? What's his face?" I snapped my fingers but couldn't bring the name to mind. "The one who had that meltdown on Instagram and posted those fucked-up videos?"

"Oh, yeah. Last time we got together for dinner with Mom and Dad, she told us all about it." He chuckled, shaking his head like he was glad she was the one who'd dealt with the spoiled little prick and not him. "And you know what she said at the time? She didn't have to like the kid. All that mattered was doing the job she was paid for, which she did. It's all blown over now, and he just got a new Netflix special."

What I was looking at was a little bigger than a Netflix special. There were plans to open offices in LA and Chicago in the pipeline. All it took was one vindictive asshole to destroy all of that.

"I can't wait to get my hands on whoever planted that fucking story." My throat tightened to the point it was difficult to speak. All I could do was seethe, staring at my glass, seeing the faces of countless suspects. Was it my fault I worked harder than the competition? Should I be held responsible for knowing how to deal with people? Getting them to trust me, understanding pain points, and how to address them? Was that something I should be vilified for? Being good at business?

"It'll be fine," Colton promised. "Sit back, relax, and let my sister do what she does best." He threw back what was left in his glass before checking his watch. "I better go. Dinner plans."

The rage boiling in my gut wasn't enough to prevent me from busting his balls. I smirked at how he hurried through, grabbing a few bills to toss on the bar. "Better hurry up, or else Rose might realize she could do better than you."

"Fuck off," he growled out.

Unlikely. "She's got you on a pretty tight leash, doesn't she?"

"I'm not complaining, am I?" That was the truth. If anything, I had never seen him so at peace. He was the same Colton I had known since the day I was born, but he was centered now—grounded—working at his father, Barrett Black's construction company, managing new projects. He is a responsible professional, when only a month ago, he'd pretty much looked down his nose at anybody who worked for a living. So long as he could get his dick wet, he was fine.

Rose was happy with him, which was what made it possible for me to accept their relationship after giving them shit for it at first. He knew I'd kill him if he ever hurt her, and that wasn't hyperbole.

The girl behind the bar lifted an eyebrow when she noticed me sitting alone after Colton made his exit. "On your own now?" she purred, leaning in and resting her forearms against the bar's surface. When she pushed them together, her tits practically spilled out over the top of her low-cut shirt. "How does a guy like you end up sitting alone at the bar?"

"Bizarre things have been known to happen," I offered with a shrug that made her giggle. She was pulling out all the stops, and I had already run the gamut from A-to-Z with every possible come-on, every attempt at seduction. If I were in a plain shitty mood after a rough day, or if I was bored or simply horny, I would have taken her up on the unspoken offer. She had the kind of body that could make a man forget his problems for at least a little while.

It wouldn't be enough.

My mind resembled a war-torn battlefield, with every thought fiercely vying for control. It had been too long since I'd had a proper night of letting go, of losing myself in the chaos of passion and desire. But tonight, the typical roll in the hay with a cute bartender would do nothing to break the tension ripping through me like barbed wire tearing at my insides.

She couldn't hide her disappointment when I added cash to Colton's already generous offering. When I dropped another hundred-dollar bill and slid the money her way, she perked up a little. "Have a good night," I offered, then left with a plan in mind.

Earlier in the week, I'd brushed off the invitation to the

masked event at Club Caramel, hand-delivered to my office in a discreet, unmarked envelope. I hadn't given it another thought until tonight while elbowing my way through the crowd, caught between wanting to scream out loud and wanting to bash somebody's face in. It didn't matter who, so long as I hurt somebody.

Nobody took what was mine. Not if they expected to live to see another day.

There had to be some way to get rid of this burning, seething rage. I'd told myself I wouldn't do it again after the first time. It was too risky for a man in my position to hang around kink clubs where anyone could recognize me, but at the moment, it was either that or kick the shit out of a random stranger whose only crime was being in my way.

Maybe a masquerade at Club Caramel was what I needed.

Dante West had a few clubs. The Vanilla Club in LA was a membership-only gentleman's club, but Club Caramel was unisex and open to the same upper-crust clientele.

It had been a while since my visit to LA, and since then, Dante had opened Club Caramel—a night of discovery. I'd found I rather enjoyed taking a dominant role during sex. Not that it was exactly a mystery. I liked having my way, calling the shots, and being in control. That had been a night to remember.

By acting as a dominant and playing with a submissive partner, a whole new world had been unlocked for me. I finally found a way to release my tension, forget everything, and wipe the slate clean. There was nothing like it for clearing my head.

That was what I needed tonight—an escape. The fact that it involved masks and disguises made the entire endeavor seem heaven-sent. The perfect opportunity for a little anonymous fun.

And if I were going to face Sienna Black in the morning, I would need a clear head. Otherwise, I'd have to kiss my business goodbye.

3

SIENNA

It wasn't unusual for me to look forward to a meeting with a new client. It was, however, unusual for me to wish I had a time machine so I could skip fifteen hours and get to the meeting that much sooner. Years spent patiently waiting for Noah Goldsmith's bullshit to bite him in the ass were finally about to pay off. And in my office, no less, even I hadn't dreamed of that added twist. Surprising, since I'd spent a lot of time dreaming of Noah's sins haunting him.

After checking off the last item on my task list, I leaned back in my chair and grinned up at the ceiling. Noah, forced to humble himself. I'd say I hoped he didn't injure himself while digging up what was left of his humility, but then that would be a lie. I wished he *had* hurt himself. He needed to be in the act of going through every single stupid, selfish choice he'd made throughout his useless life. Was he finally starting to understand he couldn't treat human beings like they were nothing but extras in the saga of his life?

That was the problem with too many guys who grew up the way we had. They all had this thing where they considered themselves the main characters, no matter where they happened to be or who they were with. Everything was about them, all the time. Even my brother, who I loved but had no illusions about. He was as selfish and thoughtless as they came and always had been.

At least, it seemed like his new relationship with Rose had mellowed him a little. It must have, or else there's no way Rose would have put up with him. I knew my best friend inside and out. She didn't suffer fools any more than I did.

If time had taught me anything, it was that Noah wouldn't mellow. If anything, he'd gotten worse over the years. He thought he was God's gift to the real estate market now, working his way to a billion, at least according to Colton. I would never bother asking or checking up on his prick of a best friend, but he'd offered the update during a dinner with our parents.

"What's this I see on your calendar?"

I looked toward the doorway to find my business partner wearing her coat, a Gucci tote hanging from the crook of her elbow. She was holding her phone out, and from a distance, I could make out the calendar entry. "Noah Goldsmith? No preliminary meeting? You're taking him on as a client without running it past me?"

I closed my eyes, wincing slightly. "You know I grew up around Noah's family. He's not a stranger. He only called this afternoon, practically begging for help, and you were out at your appointments, so we didn't have a chance to touch base on it. I'm not trying to go behind your back," I promised.

Jules scowled, but it wasn't at me. "I didn't mean to sound all confrontational. I was surprised, that's all. Is this the Noah Goldsmith whose company just bought up that property on Park Avenue?"

"The very same. He's in trouble." Did I take glee in sharing the sordid story? A little. Maybe more than a little. But I'd been waiting for this day for too long not to.

Her frown only deepened, and with it came worry lines between her brows. "Considering he is supposed to be an old family friend, you don't sound concerned."

"That would be because I'm not." Of course, that only made her more confused. "Let's just say he has this coming to him."

"That doesn't sound very promising. Are you sure you even want to help him?" She perched on the arm of a chair just inside the door, her head tipped to the side.

As always, she was graceful—an ex-dancer who had studied from an early age. It was a shame an injury had effectively ended her dreams of a dance career, but she was brilliant at business and a whiz at numbers. I would've been lost without her.

"Sure, I want to help him." It wasn't exactly the truth, but it wasn't a lie either. "He called, begging for help, and I couldn't turn him down. He knows I'm just about the only friend he has right now."

"So what's the bad blood?" When I looked at her in surprise, she waved a hand around her face before pointing to mine. "You've got this whole evil genius thing going on right now. Like if you were sitting here stroking a white cat, I wouldn't have been surprised."

I had to giggle at the image. "No, I'm not a supervillain. Although if I were, he would be my origin story."

"What happened between you two?" When I blew out a sigh, she screwed her mouth up in an expression of disapproval. "If he's going to be one of our clients, I think I deserve to know what you might be bringing to our doorstep. Know what I mean?"

I did, and it was the least I could do. "Remember, I was fifteen when this happened." With that, I launched into the story, wasting no time hitting the important points. It wasn't exactly something I liked talking about, though I had gone over it in my mind countless times over the years. Every word, every feeling, all of it was burned into my soul.

By the time I finished, she was staring at me open-mouthed. "What a fuckface!" She gasped.

A succinct conclusion. "Yeah, pretty much."

"And you've had to be around him since then? How did you manage it without killing him?"

"Family stuff. Our dads have been friends forever. Our moms too. I couldn't escape him, so I've had to play nice for ten years, at least in mixed company," I added. "Without the families around, all bets are off. He knows *exactly* how I feel."

"This is going to sound shitty." At least she warned me in advance. "Are you sure this is the right thing to do? Taking him on?"

"With the amount of money he's going to pay?" I countered with a laugh. "I'd be the world's biggest idiot if I turned down that kind of fee." And he *would* pay. He would pay through the nose.

Over the years, I'd heard too many desperate men at the end of their rope, convinced they had made the one enormous mistake they couldn't escape from. And with all his bluster and ego, Noah was as desperate as any of them. He would hand over an organ if I asked for it and would do so gladly.

That wasn't enough to convince her, judging by her deepening frown. "It's not all about money, babe."

"Well, stop everything. Am I hearing you correctly?" My

heart wasn't in it when I laughed, which came out as a hollow, haunted sort of sound.

"Laugh all you want," she muttered, shaking her head until her golden curls bounced around her shoulders. "I'm only thinking of you. You don't need to put yourself through this. That's all I'm trying to say."

"I think I do." Tapping my fingers against my desk, I imagined Noah's desperation at that very moment. "It could lead to my own closure, letting him suffer a little after what he put me through. But I'll still do my job, and I will do it damn well. You don't have to worry."

"I was never worried. Not about that." She stood and straightened out her cute little sheath dress. "Anyway, I was on my way out. I have to go home and get ready for... something."

The way she blushed and looked away piqued my interest. I needed something to think about that didn't involve Noah, which was probably why I jumped at the opportunity to change the subject. "What something?"

"Nothing."

"Well, now you have me confused. First, it was something, and now it's nothing. Which is it? Make up your mind."

"I hate it when you get like this," she grumbled, but she knew damn well I wasn't letting her off the hook until she confessed. We'd been friends for too long. "Honestly, I was going to ask if you wanted to come with me, but I didn't know if it would be your thing."

"Okay, now you're making me a little nervous."

She shook her head, giggling. "It's not like anything illegal or whatever. It's just... sort of an alternative type of evening. I got the invite a couple of weeks ago. Dante West is opening a new club here in Manhattan since the one in

California is so popular. I think I told you about the work I did for him during the summer I spent in LA."

"Dante West?" Closing my eyes, I ran through a list of names and faces in my head. It was something I had always been good at, and it helped me in my work. Wherever I went, I carried a database with me.

"Wait a second." My eyes flew open when I made the connection. "Club Caramel is a sex club, isn't it? Like, kinky sex stuff?"

Rolling her eyes, she huffed, "It's for adults who like to explore their sexuality in a safe environment."

The way she rattled it off made me laugh. "Are you filming a commercial for them? Is there a camera somewhere?" I looked around the room, still chuckling while she scowled at me.

"Hey, don't knock it until you've tried it. It's actually a lot of fun, and I've met some really cool people."

"How did I not know this about you?" We had been friends since college when we were randomly assigned as roommates my freshman year. She'd gone to LA the summer after graduation to get a little experience at a PR firm run by a cousin of hers before returning to New York to build our business.

She lifted a shoulder. "Some things are private, right? I didn't know Noah Goldsmith broke your heart, did I?"

"That's different. That's the past."

Lowering her brow, she retorted, "And I don't pry into your personal life and ask you who you sleep with."

"Bullshit," I deadpanned. "You so do."

"Okay, only because it's always obvious when you've slept with somebody new. You get all giggly and weird."

It didn't help that I hadn't slept with anybody in a

painfully long time. "So, like, what goes on at a club like this?"

Arching an eyebrow, she said, "You sound awfully interested."

I held up a finger. "Intrigued. I'm intrigued. I've heard about clubs like that, but I don't think I'd have the guts to actually go and, you know, partake."

"You would be surprised. Dante runs a very exclusive club. Everything is top quality. He's big on security and making sure nobody feels uncomfortable or forced into anything they don't want to do. You don't even have to participate," she adds. "Some people just go, have a few drinks, maybe dance a little in a sexy outfit. Then they go home. It means something different to everybody."

"You sound *very* familiar with the whole setup."

"And you sound *awfully* interested," she teased back. "You should come and see for yourself. You landed a big client today. Celebrate."

"No, I absolutely should not." The idea made me laugh helplessly. It also made me surprisingly warm and tingly down below.

What would it be like, letting loose in a sex club? There wasn't much I hadn't seen and done over the years, and I had enjoyed the handful of times a partner spanked my ass or restrained me during sex.

But a kink club? Did I have it in me to take that step?

Jules shrugged. "I'm just saying. It's a masquerade, so there's no reason to worry about being recognized. Who knows? You could end up having a good time." When I rolled my eyes in disbelief, she dropped her voice to a whisper. "There is nothing like it for clearing your head. The chance to forget who you are for one night and let loose. It's a lot of fun," she concluded. "I'm free to bring a guest if I want to. The more beautiful women at these parties, the better. I'm sure you have something short or leather you could wear, right? Something a little sexy."

Was I honestly considering this? Already, a plan was beginning to take shape in my head. There were a handful of shops where I'd easily be able to find a mask to cover half of my face. "I do have a few dresses in my closet that might work," I mused, chewing my lip.

"People wear whatever they feel like wearing," she assured me. "I think you could have a great time. Live a little. You work so hard, Sienna."

"Are you saying I need to loosen up?"

"Don't take it personally," she mused. "But yeah, you could stand to chill, especially with that complete asshole coming in tomorrow. You'd be surprised how easy it is to deal with life when your ass is still sore from last night... among other places," she added, wiggling her eyebrows up and down.

"I'm not getting my ass spanked tonight," I insisted. "I'm going to go, have a little fun, and that's it. I need to turn in early."

"Sure, sure." She tapped something on her phone moments before my phone buzzed. "There's the address. I'll meet you there at ten." She was gone before I had time for second thoughts. Granted, if I changed my mind, I could always text her and let her know. I didn't *have* to show up at the club.

At the same time, I got my things together and flipped off the lights with a spring in my step that wasn't there before. Not even the idea of putting Noah in his place could make me tingle the way the idea of walking around anonymously in a sex club did.

Jules was right. Considering the thought of him set my

teeth on edge, it would be best if I worked out a little tension tonight. Whether that meant getting my drink on while dancing or hooking up with a hot stranger was anybody's guess.

One thing was for sure. By the time I reached the lobby of our building, I was determined to meet Jules at the club. There were only so many one-time-only offers a girl got in her life. I couldn't afford to pass it up.

4

NOAH

Anticipation.

It practically crackled, almost shimmering around me.

I knew it was a risk being here, but the fact it was a masquerade ball lessened that. I wouldn't be recognized, and there was no avoiding the excitement in the air. Then again, that might have been the effect of a couple of drinks plus the elaborate lighting throughout the club.

I was hardly a stranger to this kind of establishment, but Dante had pulled out all the stops for this opening event. He wanted to stand out from the pack and provide an exclusive experience, something high-class, without the sketchy reputation such clubs could easily earn themselves.

Before leaving the lobby, all guests were required to surrender their devices—no chance of anyone taking pictures. I could appreciate the rule, even if I was already a little twitchy, patting the pockets of my black slacks in an unconscious effort to locate the phone. Being here made me uneasy, but the fact no one could identify me and have proof was another reason why I had convinced myself I couldn't get caught there.

If I was distracted enough to think about that, it meant I wasn't invested in the activity going on around me—not a good sign. I was too busy waiting for word to spread of the bullshit rumors with my name attached to them, waiting for the texts and phone calls.

Sienna knew why I was calling before I had a chance to explain, telling me it was only a matter of time before everyone in my life found out before a single word was published.

Rather than looking at this evening as an opportunity to escape that, my attention was locked in a box elsewhere in the club. In other words, it was pretty pathetic.

A curvy blonde nudged me accidentally on purpose as she leaned in to call her order out to the bartender. "Sorry," she offered, her glossy lips curving into an inviting smile. She wore a mask that covered most of her face, and her green eyes stood out bright against the black lace ringing them. "Big night, huh? Have you ever been to one of Mr. West's clubs before?"

Looking over the top of her head, I caught sight of the man in question standing near the doorway leading from the lobby. He wore a mask the way his guests did, but unlike the rest of us, he wore a tuxedo and made a point of warmly greeting everyone who entered. His hospitality was legendary, but at heart, he was a businessman. He knew what his clientele needed and went out of his way to provide for them.

"Once or twice, out on the West Coast," I told the anonymous woman beside me. "But this is twice the size of Club Vanilla, at least at first glance." Fuck, I was standing in a kink club with an interested, half-naked blonde next to me, and I sounded like I was moments away from discussing square footage.

She didn't seem to mind, swaying closer, her tongue darting over her lips. "What are you into?" Cutting straight to the chase, it came as no surprise.

I'd been there for an hour and had already witnessed more than a few couples grinding openly on the dance floor. A handful of guests had slipped into the rooms ringing the floor's perimeter, where various scenes were playing out for everyone to observe.

At midnight, a show would take place in the center of the dance floor. From what I'd overheard, it would involve elaborate rope bondage. That wasn't really my preference, but I always enjoyed watching a woman being restrained and forced to receive pleasure.

"A lot of things," I replied, and some of the light faded from her eyes. She didn't do it for me—plain and simple— though I did enjoy the sight of her mostly exposed ass as she walked away, approaching another potential partner.

It wasn't that there was anything wrong with her. There was nothing wrong with any of the beautiful bodies around me, all of them at least partially naked. The blonde would easily find an eager partner who wanted what she was offering. I would've bet my net worth that virtually every flavor of kink and preference was on display.

For instance, a tall, latex-clad woman in knee-high spiked boots led a man on all fours, his head covered completely by a black leather mask to which his leash was attached. For all I knew, he could have been a client of mine or maybe an associate.

Servers wearing revealing French lingerie moved about carrying trays loaded with champagne to celebrate the club opening. I decided to stick to whiskey, shaking my head to decline an offer. Unlike many of the people around me, I wasn't exactly in costume, sticking to a black button-down to match my slacks and a black leather mask that concealed the upper half of my face. Some people got off on dressing up, male and female, forgetting who they were in favor of being who they secretly longed to be.

Normally, I wouldn't want to be anyone but who I was. Why would I need to pretend? I had everything and was hardly what anyone would call repressed.

Tonight was a different story. There was a storm building in me, swirling dangerously close to the shore. I needed to escape, but I had yet to find anyone or anything enticing enough to get me out of my own head.

I stalked around the space like a restless lion, my attention brushing over one scene after another. Both the dance floor and the seating areas were open for public play, and things were heating up now that alcohol had been flowing.

A pair of blondes kissed passionately on a long, leather bench while the men they were with stroked their legs and cocks. I glanced through the door to one of the side rooms and found a big guy who could've passed for one of the bouncers bent over a chair, having his bare ass flogged by a tall, imposing brunette who used a flogger like it was an extension of her arm. What a shame I wasn't into having my ass flogged since I appreciated the professionalism, and she was clearly devoted to her craft.

Some people craved a little humiliation, even in front of a crowd. I preferred control and couldn't imagine handing it over to even a trusted partner, especially not with a dozen curious bystanders getting off on the action.

I moved on, increasingly uncomfortable. Not even the sights and sounds of foreplay were enough to take my mind off my troubles. I might have been better off going out and scoring pussy at one of the usual bars I frequented with my friends. I had never failed once I set my sights on a new plaything.

I was on the fence about whether I wanted to stay or go when a bubblegum pink wig caught my eye. A few women wore wigs to further the disguise, and hers was an attention-getter for sure. She was medium height, taller thanks to a pair of heels that had to be at least four inches and roughly as thick as pencils. She handled them with ease, maneuvering her way through the crowd without missing a step.

Once the throng of bodies parted, I noticed the tiny girl walking with her. She wore a jet black wig, so long it brushed her ass, but the pink bob held my interest. There was no reason why, exactly. Between the wig and the mask, there wasn't much I could discern about the woman's identity. Yet her glistening, ruby lips were the first to draw my hungry stare all evening.

It took a few minutes of observing her before I understood why she drew my attention from so many other gorgeous bodies and willing smiles. She was an innocent fawn, almost trembling though she did her damnedest to hide it. She paused in the doorway I had recently left, where the big guy was earning stripes across his ass with every sharp slap of the flogger. Her ruby mouth fell open before snapping shut, followed by a furtive glance around to see whether anybody had noticed her shock. The apples of her cheeks went pink before she scurried away while her friend entered the room to get a closer look.

Satisfaction spread through me like warm honey, loosening my joints and muscles, calming the storm. The fawn was on her own, surrounded by predators. Whether or not she saw it that way, that was the situation in a nutshell. I noticed one, then two men turn their heads to check her out. An hourglass figure, perfectly encased in a black dress cut short enough to flirt with the curve of her ass cheeks. Every step she took hinted at a flash of plump flesh but never quite delivered. Long, smooth legs encased in black stockings with seams running up the back, a detail I always admired. She was hypnotic, her hips swaying slightly as she carefully made her way around.

One of the men made a move like he was thinking of approaching her, but I cut him off before he could take a step.

No, she was mine.

No one had to say it.

I knew it.

She was who I was there for, this innocent thing who probably thought she was sophisticated and worldly outside these walls. After all, Dante West's circle of friends and clients was impressive. She had to be *somebody*—a model, maybe, or an actress. With a body like that, she could've done anything, and what little I'd seen of her face left no doubt in my mind of her beauty.

Now, I was the hunter, and she was the prey. Stalking her through the crowd, watching from a distance as she watched a pair of men grind against the curvy blonde between them. She stared, openly fascinated. I wanted to know why. What was it about their erotic dancing that brought her to a dead stop? Did she imagine herself as the lucky girl whose body was sandwiched between men whose hands ran over her tits and ass? Was this something she fantasized about when she was alone? Would she touch herself later, remembering the way the blonde's moans rang out over the music and conversation around us? Would she take the blonde's place and imagine her own hands were the hands of these men?

Not if I gave her something worth remembering.

My dick was aching, throbbing by the time I decided to move closer. There was no other choice. A force stronger than me pulled me across the floor. I needed to touch her. To educate her.

Countless warm bodies brushed against mine as I passed, focused on my goal. They no longer existed. Everything had ceased to exist the second I decided she would be mine, whoever she was.

She must have felt my presence, turning and lifting her head before I reached her side. Clear, blue eyes flashed a mixture of uncertainty and arousal, locking onto mine and holding me in place for a heartbeat or two. It was only us, brought together by something unseen but extremely potent. I longed for the touch of her creamy skin, to indulge in the full tits that were barely held back by her skimpy dress. I needed to feel her shatter around me. There was nothing like a whiff of vulnerability to turn me into a fucking beast, and she was so vulnerable.

My eyes scanned the area behind her, where a handful of doors lined up along the far wall, representing private rooms where two or more consenting adults could play without prying eyes watching every move. I needed her to myself. Just for tonight, just until her delicious submission wiped away every last worry.

I inclined my head toward one of the rooms whose door stood open. She looked that way over her shoulder, and in the crisscrossing beams of light from high above the floor, I caught sight of her teeth sinking into her lip. Doubtful. Worried.

I extended a hand in silent invitation. I wouldn't speak. The decision wasn't a conscious one—pure self-preservation, nothing more. What if she recognized my voice? What a time to be discovered in a sex club, even if my partner might have as much to lose as I did. Besides, there was so much that could be conveyed without the use of words.

She hesitated, eyeing my hand, biting her lip harder. It was no use, though. She knew as well as I did what needed to happen. That was why she placed her hand in mine and allowed me to lead her across the floor, winding our way through the crowd, past kissing, groping guests. Kids play compared to what I had in mind.

Thank fuck I hadn't left.

5

SIENNA

This was crazy.

This was absolutely crazy.

First, Jules had basically abandoned me to watch some guy getting whipped or whatever was happening. I was too nervous to keep watching.

Obviously, the nerves had worn off. Now, I was allowing myself to be led to a small, dark room away from the main floor by a stranger, no less, one who hadn't said a word. All it had taken was his hand outstretched in my direction, and I was basically his.

It hadn't occurred to me to say no.

I can still say no.

Sure, that was an option, and all things considered, it was probably the best course of action.

I didn't have to do this.

I didn't have to do anything.

But I wanted to.

That was the most surprising part of all—how much I wanted this. It was the mystery of it all. Who was he? What brought him to the party? And why, out of so many beautiful women he could have chosen, did he choose me?

I wasn't stupid. I knew I looked good in a YSL dress that was too short and tight to wear in public. It showed off my body, which I worked at keeping in shape, and my strappy Versace stilettos made my legs look incredible. But I didn't walk around with the kind of confidence I'd seen from so many people ever since we walked through the door and handed over our phones.

These weren't first-timers. I must've stuck out like a sore thumb, feeling awkward and out of place. Maybe that was why he wanted me. Because I seemed naïve. Some men got off on that, just like some got off on people watching them getting their asses whipped.

All I knew was that by the time we stepped inside that windowless room, there was something indescribable about him and about the way his touch made me feel. I slowly stepped into the center of the room, eyeing the toys hanging along one wall—paddles, floggers, whips. Underneath it was a table full of toys that made my stomach flutter and my core heat.

I wasn't a stranger to sex toys and had a few in my bedside table, but I didn't recognize half of what I saw.

Suddenly, everything was very real, and my heart caught in my throat before I turned to find the stranger closing the door. He was so tall, broad-shouldered, with thick arms and hands that could crush me. It would be the two of us. Alone. And there was no way I could fight him off if things went south. "I'm—" I croaked.

He held a finger to his lips, shaking his head. So that was how he wanted to play it.

It wasn't how I wanted it. "But—" I insisted, folding my arms over my trembling body.

For a man of his size, he moved fast. Not that the room was very big, but it still took my breath away at how suddenly he was in front of me with his huge hand holding the back of my neck. I gasped, caught between surprise and alarm, before he touched the index finger of his free hand to my lips. "Shh..." he whispered, dragging out the sound and cutting off any objection ready to leave my lips.

There was something strangely erotic about it, something in his commanding presence that melted my worries. My heart beat wildly, and I had to remind myself to breathe as the stranger traced my lips, then slid over my chin and down my throat. I shuddered involuntarily as tiny sparks of sensation sizzled their way through me, becoming more intense the lower his finger dipped.

A deep growl stirred in his throat before he released a shaky breath, his gaze lowering until he was staring at my heaving chest. Another growl rumbled as he reached for my hand, closing his fingers around my wrist before pressing my palm to his enormous bulge. I sucked in a quick gasp at the size of it, not to mention how forward and commanding he was. He didn't have to say a word for me to understand his meaning, although his gaze held mine for what? Consent?

Now was the time to leave.

Fuck no.

I nodded and could hardly believe what I was doing, but it was like I wasn't in charge of my actions anymore. Something bigger than me had taken over, and that force made me rub him in slow, deliberate circles. His dark eyes—all I could see of the top half of his face thanks to a black leather mask—closed for a second while he growled again. It was a powerful sound, enough to make the fine hairs on the nape of my neck stand on end.

I was hanging in midair, caught between apprehension and the indescribable thrill of being caught up at that moment with him.

His finely sculpted lips parted so he could let out a throaty whisper. "Down." The hand on the back of my neck tightened before he applied downward pressure that forced me to my knees in front of him. His dick was at eye-level now, jutting straight out from his slacks. Hunger roared in me, making me lick my lips before I lifted my gaze to find him staring down at me. He could've done anything he wanted at that moment, the two of us alone in that room.

The uncertainty only heightened the anticipation that already had me hot and wet.

"Take it out," he rasped over the slow beat of music. The command stole my breath, my fingers trembling as I worked his belt. Somehow, there was relief in being told what to do. I didn't have to think. I only had to obey, and I did, wasting no time opening his slacks and letting them fall around his ankles. That left a pair of tight boxer briefs expertly outlining his enormous package. I slid my hands up his thick, bulging thighs, savoring his soft groan of approval before sliding my fingers beneath the waistband and lowering his shorts.

I was doing this.

I was allowing a stranger to feed me his cock, guiding the head to my lips. The bead of precum on his tip was visible even in the dim light, a slightly salty tang exploding on my tongue when I greedily licked it up.

He sighed and stroked the cheap wig I had bought for tonight. "Good girl," he whispered, and my body went warm all over, thanks to his praise.

Who knew I had a thing for that? I was already learning so much about myself tonight.

The heat in my body and the pleasure his praise stirred up made me bolder. I extended my tongue again, this time swirling it around the thick ridge until he took me by the back of my head and forced me down, pushing his cock into my mouth until he hit the back of my throat. So big and thick. I released a whimper and gagged before he loosened his grip so I could come up for air. I was barely able to take more than half of him, and I had to use my hand to make up for the difference.

Here I was, on my knees, letting this man use me. It was wrong, but there was something freeing about it at the same time—I could let go and follow my body's desires. No complications. No promises. Nothing but letting things happen and allowing him to take control.

The sounds of his rapid breathing were a symphony, making me move faster, bobbing my head while he slid in and out of my mouth. The sound and the feel of him made my juices flow until they coated my bare lips, dampening my lace panties.

I couldn't help but moan around him, excited and frustrated all at once. I needed relief from the almost painful throbbing of my clit, and it only got worse when he groaned helplessly.

Even on my knees, I had power over this towering man.

This sort of power was new.

Hot.

Something I wanted more of.

His hand tightened around the back of my head to hold me in place before his hips began jerking faster so he could fuck my face. There was nothing for me to do but brace myself against his thick thighs and struggle to breathe. "Take it," he whispered between thrusts, and I did. I was proud of myself for doing it and not breaking. No, in fact, by the time he pulled out so I could gasp for air, I was practically glowing with pride and burning with need. Dying for relief.

His glistening dick swayed in my face before he pulled me to my feet without warning and ran his hands down my sides and over my ass. His throaty rasp rang in my ears. "Good girl."

I whimpered softly in response while my body sang under his caress. God, it was electric, every touch making me want more. By the time he turned me in place and nudged me up against the toy table, I was weak and willing to do anything he wanted.

With one leg, he parted mine, spreading my thighs and bending me over until I propped myself up on my forearms. What was he going to do? The anticipation was damn close to killing me as one moment followed another, with only his ragged breathing piercing the silence.

I released a long sigh when his hands touched my ankles, arching my back and spreading my legs wider as he began making his way up my stocking-covered calves. *Fuck, so good.* My throaty moan was cut off when he clamped a hand over my mouth before continuing. It was so sinful and dirty, but there wasn't a single part of me that wanted to stop.

I would die if he stopped.

His breath hitched when his fingers brushed over the scrap of lace covering my throbbing mound. My knees threatened to buckle, but I held myself up, forcing myself to endure what was starting to feel like torture. It was almost too much to take, the sensations assaulting me from all directions. The smell of his cologne, the heat from his skin, the way his fingers danced over my aching flesh until my nerves sizzled, and I was ready to beg for relief.

Nothing in the world mattered as much as ending this torment.

With a sudden, sharp jerk, he tore my panties away. I barely registered the sound of tearing stitches before the balled-up fabric was forced into my mouth as his thick digits plunged inside me. Shock melted into blistering pleasure, the friction from his fingers pressed against my G-spot, taking what was already bubbling inside me and turning it into boiling, blistering, primal lust. Rather than spit the panties out, I let them muffle my moans, pushing back against his strokes, frantic to come.

I was close, out of my mind between his pumping fingers and grunts close to my ear. "You like that?" he whispered, running his tongue along the seashell curve of my ear while I moaned my approval.

I could taste myself on the lace, and that realization—the dirtiness of it, how filthy it was—took me over the edge.

His satisfied groans filled my ears as one spasm after another rolled through me. It went on and on, and so did he, still pumping in and out of my quivering hole, this time adding a thumb against my clit. "Yes," he rasped in my ear when I jerked in response. His whispers were the only thing tethering me to consciousness. "Let it go. Come for me."

I was coming again. I might not ever have stopped. By the time he withdrew his fingers and patted my ass, I was limp across the table, shaking and weakly whimpering. "Good girl," he whispered.

My head was still spinning by the time his legs touched mine. A second later, I heard a packet tear. A condom. I could barely move, dizzy, almost afraid of how hard I came like I didn't know my own body. I didn't know I was capable of that.

But even though I was damn near destroyed and still

coming down from my high, I nodded at the pressure against my pussy when he ran his head through my sensitive folds. Even though my throat was raw, I moaned my approval.

I still wanted more.

I wanted all of him.

I wanted everything he had to give.

And he gave it to me, not bothering to be gentle or cautious now that he'd stretched me with his fingers. They were nothing compared to his wide head and the way it stretched me when he pushed deep enough and hard enough to rock me against the table, knocking a few of the toys to the floor.

He settled in, his thighs against my ass with my dress worked up around my hips. I barely had the chance to adjust to him before he pulled back and filled me again. I could only moan to tell him how much I loved it, and he rewarded me with a sharp slap against my ass.

I gasped, jerking, but the sublime warmth left me wanting more. He scraped his fingers against my throbbing flesh before delivering a blow against my other cheek.

It was too much. I couldn't take any more. My senses were overloaded, the tension in my core unbearable. Before I knew it, I was coming, reaching the crest of the wave and tumbling over the top. The force pulled me down, submerging me in darkness into perfect bliss. I couldn't hear anything but my heart beating in my ears, but somewhere in the middle of all of it, I sensed him driving himself into me one last time and letting go.

All it took was him pulling back and stepping away for me to sink to the floor before large hands caught me and readied me upright. I gripped the wall, too weak to hold myself up anymore, still trembling, fighting to catch my breath. I'd never come that hard, not even close. Until now, I hadn't known my body was capable of it.

Spitting out the panties, I pulled in a deep breath before chuckling a little at myself. Now that it was over, I was coming back to my senses. The spell was broken, but that was okay. I was grateful. A little embarrassed, maybe, but grateful.

"That was... unexpected." I looked up, still chuckling, but the sound died when I realized I was alone. He had left without a word, not even a sound. If it wasn't for the throbbing in my core, I might have wondered if he was real or if I'd made the whole thing up.

It was probably for the best, no matter how my heart sank. I didn't know what to say or what the protocol was. I probably would have ended up ruining things by saying something awkward.

Though I did sort of wish there was a way for us to see each other again. Because I was pretty sure he had ruined me for all other men.

6

NOAH

The bitch was keeping me waiting.

I shifted in my chair, silently seething as one minute after another ticked past. So this was the game she wanted to play? I had gone out of my way to make it to her office on time, only to sit outside her closed door while a nerdy-looking girl who was probably fresh out of college gave me a sympathetic grimace. "I'm sure she'll only be another few minutes," she insisted. "Are you sure there's nothing I can get for you? Some coffee? A bottle of Evian?"

What I could have used was a stiff drink, something to blunt my irritation before I had no choice but to kick the door down. There wasn't much I hated more than petty mind games, and starting off this way didn't bode well for what was to come. The blinds covering the windows looking into Sienna's office were drawn, giving me no hint as to what she was doing. She might have been on a call, but she could just as easily have been sitting back and laughing, knowing she was holding the strings. I had no choice but to dance if I didn't want to lose everything.

How much worse would I be if I hadn't purged my anger

last night? Sure, I was irritated as fuck, sitting with my thumb up my ass, waiting for Sienna Black to decide to grace me with her presence. But even that was a mild irritation when yesterday afternoon, I would have torn the place apart out of sheer rage.

I should have gotten the girl's name. A stupid thought, childish. It was the right decision, leaving when I did. Better to stay anonymous, even if it meant I didn't take the time to check in with her. I didn't trust myself to walk away once the façade dropped, and we were nothing but two people who'd just finished coming until they couldn't see straight.

I knew there was no choice but to leave when I had, but it didn't stop me from wishing we had done more. Her pussy's aroma hadn't left my memory in the hours since I smelled her on my fingers. Ambrosial enough to make my cock twitch while waiting for my meeting to start. She came so exquisitely, shaking and weak. A smile had stirred my lips when I felt her limp body in my arms while helping her to her feet.

What a time for a soft alarm to sound. Sienna's assistant looked up from her MacBook, this time wearing a smile. "Miss Black will see you now," she chirped. I expected her to get up, but she only returned her attention to whatever she was working on. It wouldn't have surprised me in the least to find out Sienna told her to let me see myself in. She wouldn't want to be cordial or welcoming.

Gritting my teeth, I stood and went to the door. At least her shitty attitude meant the end of the semi that had been growing in my pants. I'd have plenty of time to reflect on last night once the meeting was over.

And if the meeting went terribly, I would have all the time in the world since I would lose my business and personal reputation. I held that image in my mind as I opened the heavy oak door and entered the large, sunlight-drenched corner office.

Good thing I hadn't expected a warm welcome since I didn't receive one. "You look a lot better than I expected this morning." That was her idea of a greeting, delivered in a snide tone that left me biting my tongue. It would've been too satisfying in the moment to tell her to fuck herself.

"What makes you say that?" I asked, forcing a brittle smile as I closed the door behind me. *Do not fuck this up.* She probably craved nothing more than the satisfaction of knowing I couldn't bear working with her.

"I imagined you'd stumble in here, bleary-eyed and miserable." Looking me up and down, she clicked her tongue in what could've been disappointment. "I'm sure it's for the best you didn't drink yourself half to death last night. Have a seat."

Sienna remained seated, watching closely as I approached. Barely a muscle on her face twitched as I unbuttoned my charcoal gray jacket and sat across from her, but not before pointedly checking my watch. "Busy day?" I asked.

"You should know how unpredictable work can sometimes be. Last-minute emergencies, that sort of thing." There was nothing remotely close to sorrow in her voice, not that I expected it. So far, she was behaving much like I expected. There was a chip on her shoulder that had only gotten bigger as the years passed.

What a shame she had to act like such a bitch, since she was drop-dead gorgeous and couldn't hide the killer body under her sleek pantsuit. Then again, it could've been for the best. Her bitchy attitude killed any boners before they could stir and kept me out of Colton's crosshairs.

Could I have brought up that stupid prank and cleared

the air? I might have tried, but I doubted I would've been successful. Besides, it would've looked pathetic to dredge up the past. Like I was scrambling to get in her good graces now that she held a scrap of power over me. That wasn't going to happen. Not in this lifetime.

Wearing an expression of mock sadness, Sienna rotated her laptop, allowing me a look at the ugly article that had gone live overnight. *"Manhattan Real Estate Tycoon Noah Goldsmith's Business Practices Called Into Question,"* she recited, quoting the subheading. "Really, this isn't as ugly as I expected."

Considering I practically knew the damn article by heart, having gone over it with a fine-tooth comb at least two dozen times since waking up, I could only snort weakly at her statement. "Easy for you to say. It isn't your integrity and reputation on the line."

"All I'm saying is, let's keep a sense of realism. It's ugly," she admitted in a way that left me feeling like she was throwing me a bone. "But it's not anything we can't rise above. It will take a little careful maneuvering, that's all."

As she spoke, my phone buzzed. I ignored it, though the vibration reminded me of the stakes. Probably another call from a concerned associate or, worse, another call from my sister, Rose, or one of my parents. They were concerned, but it felt a lot more like disappointment to me. I could see through their assurances and could hear the emptiness behind their words. Like everyone else, they thought I was getting what was coming to me.

At least, that was very much how it seemed.

"I'm in your hands," I told her, no matter how uncomfortable the notion made me.

And she knew it too.

She sat back in her chair, lips twitching. I was used to

that smart-ass expression after having it thrown my way countless times. She always acted like she knew something the rest of us didn't, which irritated me into adding, "I hope you know what you're doing. Have you ever handled a client like me before?"

I knew I was in for it when she arched an eyebrow. Her blue eyes sparkled, but there was nothing joyful in them. There was more malice behind that glow. Her chocolate waves glistened in the sunlight as she turned her head, gazing through the window beside her. "What do you think of the view?" she asked, deflecting my question.

That was the thing. From where I sat, the view wasn't bad at all. Sienna looked a hell of a lot like her mom, Lourde, who happened to be my first crush. Nobody knew that, not even Colton. Looking at Sienna now, I admired the same delicate bone structure, her long, graceful neck, and pouty lips that pursed while she was deep in thought, the way they did now. I cleared my throat and glanced out the window before I could forget who I was looking at and start thinking very bad, dirty things. "It's nice."

"Tell me the truth. Do you think I could have ended up in this office without knowing what I'm doing? And before you make an ass out of yourself..." she added with a sharp look, "... I did this on my own. No help."

Something told me her last name and her parents' ties had a little something to do with it, but I couldn't risk getting thrown out. Swallowing my irritation, I grunted my understanding.

"I know what I'm doing, Noah. Unlike you, I have an excellent reputation. I'd be more than happy to give you the contact information for a few of my most recent clients, though, if that would make you feel better. But between you and me, I don't think we have that kind of time."

"Which is it?" I folded my hands, lowering my brow. "Will this be easy to overcome, or are we in trouble?"

"Two things can be true at once," she retorted in a sickeningly sweet voice. One thing was for sure—she spent much too much time with my sister, to the point where they had adopted some of each other's annoying habits. In a way, Sienna was like a sister, albeit one who hated my guts. The fact that she was stunningly gorgeous was secondary.

She sat up straighter, rolling her shoulders back. I took a moment to appreciate the slim cut of her powder blue suit jacket before she rattled off items from a list on her screen. "The way I see it, there are two options of attack. First, you have the option of issuing a response to these claims. Have you received any calls or messages from the press asking for your thoughts?"

"Are you kidding?" As we spoke, my phone buzzed again. "I don't bother answering unknown numbers, and that's virtually all I've seen all morning. I haven't bothered to listen to the voicemails."

"Forward everything to me... names, phone numbers, text messages, emails. I want all of it. You don't have to worry about a thing." She spoke quickly, completely self-assured. To her, this was another day at the office.

"It's as simple as that?" I couldn't help but feel skeptical, especially considering our history. "You're going to handle all of it?"

"That's what you're paying me for," she reminded me. "Let's face it. We don't need you shooting yourself in the foot by making some jackass statement."

She was determined to torture me. Still, the idea of being able to ignore the harassment wasn't bad.

"In case you're looking for an expert opinion, it's better to keep any rebuttal short and sweet. Something like this."

She cleared her throat, then read from her screen. "Mr. Goldsmith is deeply troubled by the accusations made by an anonymous source. It pains him to be denied the opportunity to face his accuser, but he is firm in his unequivocal denial."

"That doesn't sound bad," I had to admit.

"Yeah, well, it's not my first rodeo." Still, she was frowning when she looked away from the computer. "I need one thing from you."

"You mean besides a paid invoice?"

She didn't bother pretending to enjoy my joke. "Are the accusations false?"

I winced, feigning injury. "That hurts."

"I doubt it," she fired back, unflinching, unblinking. "I need to know. If I release this statement, is it the truth? I am not about to destroy my professional integrity for you."

Indignation flared in my chest. So much for the sense of peace I had enjoyed after my night at the club. "You know it's not true."

"No. I don't know if it's not true. And don't get all pissy on me," she snapped when I rolled my eyes. "Don't act like you're some saint who would never swing his dick around like it's the first prize for a lucky winner. You've been pretty free and easy when it comes to who you sleep with. Is it really surprising knowing people might wonder how much of a story like this is true? You mean to tell me you've never slept with anybody you've done business with?"

"I don't shit where I eat."

She stared at me expectantly before frowning. "That's all you have to say? *You don't shit where you eat?*"

That was the most I trusted myself to say. She had no idea how much self-restraint I was practicing, bearing the weight of her judgment. "I'm not interested in getting into semantics with you," I replied as evenly as I could. "I said it, I meant it. That's going to have to be enough."

"So I won't be telling a lie when I deny this on your behalf."

"That's right." I maintained eye contact, refusing to look away. I wouldn't give her the satisfaction.

With a short nod, she pulled her computer closer before typing. "If you approve of the verbiage, then we'll go public with the statement."

"I have to hand it to you," I observed while she tapped on her keyboard. "You can be pretty cold when you feel like it."

"I'm sorry." Her fingers continued to move over her keyboard after she turned her attention to me. It was unnerving as fuck. "Am I supposed to weep and wail? Shake my fist at how cruel the world can be? If that's what you're looking for, you came to the wrong place and need to find a new public relations genius to handle this for you."

"Genius?" I muttered before snickering. "Let's not give ourselves more credit than we deserve."

"Keep talking," she invited, abandoning her MacBook and turning her full attention to me. "Talk your way out of this life-saving assistance I'm offering. And enjoy trying to explain it to everyone because I'll be damned if I make excuses for your poor decisions to the people we know."

"Right. Enough." She was giving me a headache. I rubbed the bridge of my nose, grunting. "Just tell me what you need me to do so we can get this over with."

"Keep your social calendar clear. I'm going to line up a few events where you can make appearances."

"Like what?" I groaned.

"Charity events, first and foremost. That's the low-hanging fruit. Beyond that, what do you think about setting up a sports clinic for underprivileged kids? An event where a handful of pros meet up with them, take a few photos, and show them how to swing a bat. That kind of thing. It will all have your name on it." She waved a hand. "I'll deal with the details."

"Whatever. As long as I don't have to spend much time with the brats."

"Way to go," she muttered. "Be sure to say something like that in public. That's the kind of attitude people consider likable."

"I don't give a shit if I'm—" I caught myself before I finished the statement, but it was too late.

"Yeah, no kidding," she chortled. "Hence, you being in this position. For what it's worth, I would also like to find out who planted this story. Any idea who it might've been?"

Because it was what she already believed, I snapped, "It'll take some time for me to compile a list of people I've fucked over." With that, I stood and buttoned my jacket. "You have this under control. I'll forward you the names, numbers, all that shit." If I spent another minute with her, I'd destroy everything. She was an expert at pushing my buttons, almost like she'd spent years honing her skills. For all I knew, she had.

"Do us both a favor and keep your mouth shut," she warned as I left her office. "I'm a genius, but I'm not a miracle worker."

"I could think of a few other words to describe you." Her face fell in the split second I closed the door between us. It gave me almost as much pleasure as anything I'd experienced at the club.

7

SIENNA

Why? Why do I let him get under my skin?

Noah was long gone, and I sat staring at the closed door with my fists clenched in my lap. I told myself I wouldn't let him irk me and would keep it professional, no jabs, no barbs. Nothing about this had to be personal. It was a job.

I was good at my job.

I loved my job.

But when it came to him, all bets were off.

I released a shuddering breath and consciously let go of the tension that had tightened into a knot at the nape of my neck. All I needed was to end up with a migraine because of him. I kept that in mind as I took a few slow, deep breaths until, finally, my muscles loosened and the pounding in my head lessened.

At least he hadn't fought me. He could bitch and moan all he wanted, but facts were facts. He was at the mercy of public opinion right now, which left him at *my* mercy. He may have been talented at some things. I hated him, but I wasn't naïve. Nobody built a business the size of his if they didn't at least know a thing or two about how to earn trust and turn a profit. He wasn't what anyone would call a people person, yet at the same time, he understood people. He knew what they needed to see and hear.

So why was he in this spot? He made a sarcastic joke about being unable to identify everybody he had fucked over, and I had to wonder how much of it was true. Because there was another side to the success coin. A man on his way to his first billion didn't normally get there without having fucked over at least one or two people along the way. Undercutting them on a deal, maybe making a few sketchy investments.

I typed the word *investment* in the document I'd opened to compile thoughts and ideas, along with it was a mess of other notes I'd jotted down in the minutes and hours after Noah's phone call. At the heart of it all was the question of who had planted the story and why.

Was it wrong that I almost felt sorry for whoever they were? Nobody went that route unless they had been good and thoroughly fucked by somebody. I knew the feeling too well. Hell, there was a part of me that wanted to shake their hand, whoever they were. At least they had tried to strike back. All I had been able to do was bear the humiliation, which I was unfortunately reminded of every time I came into contact with Noah in the years since that awful night.

I sat back in my chair with a sigh, my thoughts now on anything but the job at hand. Staring out the window, I no longer saw the striking high rises around me or the East River in the distance. I saw Penelope Schwartz's snide smirk.

She hadn't kicked my ass the way she'd threatened, probably because she knew better than to try. The school's administration had looked the other way on a lot of things because there wasn't a single student there whose parents didn't wield influence. But even they knew where to draw a line and punish bad behavior. Besides, Penelope had practically been royalty around there, and she'd had a reputation to uphold as student body president along with half a dozen clubs. Beating up a freshman would have put an end to her shiny image.

Even years later, I shivered thinking about it. Going to school with my heart in my throat, expecting to be taunted and bullied. Shriveling under the weight of Penelope's gaze whenever we passed in the halls. It was all thanks to that cruel, arrogant bastard. He had never even apologized. My brother's best friend, someone I'd known my entire life, and he hadn't apologized.

My jaw ached thanks to the way I ground my teeth. My dentist was going to have a few choice words for me at my next appointment if I wasn't careful. I deliberately loosened my jaw, chiding myself. Noah did not deserve this power over me.

My phone buzzed with an alert, quickly followed by a soft ping from my computer—an appointment reminder. I was never so glad for a distraction to pull me out of my murderous thoughts. My cousin, Aria, had talked me into signing up for a spin class with Skye Worthington, one of the hottest instructors on the East Side. God knew I needed the endorphins, and Aria's mom, Evelyn, swore by Skye's classes. Considering she had the body of a woman my age and my Uncle Magnus still looked at her like he wanted to ravish her, I was sold.

I stood from my desk and crossed the room, ducking into the attached bathroom to change into my workout clothes before heading to the spin studio. I needed to get rid of this nasty energy wrapped around me like the thin, sticky strands of a spiderweb. The harder I fought, the more stuck I became. If I weren't careful, I would end up paralyzed by the spider at the center of it all.

Marissa looked up from her work when I emerged from my office, now dressed in workout gear. "Spin class?" she asked, privy to my schedule.

I nodded, looking across the floor. The dozens of employees Jules managed were hard at work, typing up press releases, managing social media accounts, confirming reservations, and basically making the entire company run. I was under no illusions. I might have been the wizard behind the curtain, pulling levers and pushing buttons, but they kept the gears moving.

"I'll oversee all communication on the Goldsmith account," I announced to my assistant, whose eyes widened slightly with surprise. "This is one I would like to handle on my own."

"That works," she murmured in a way that told me she didn't think it worked at all. "I guess I shouldn't be surprised, with you two knowing each other. It's personal."

Yes, it was definitely personal. "I know how to handle him," I explained with a wink. Her concern softened thanks to that, which is why I had done it. I couldn't have her questioning my motivation or wondering if my management of this client was a smart move. I already had Jules concerned over that as it was.

Passing Jules' closed office door on my way to the elevator, I frowned when I remembered her wandering off at the club. Granted, it wasn't like we had promised to stick close to each other, but I had felt hopelessly out of place and more than a little intimidated. I hadn't seen her after slinking out of that little room with my panties shoved down the front of my dress, though, to be fair, I was in a hurry to get home after that. My whole world had turned on its head. I had needed time to decompress and figure out what the hell happened.

Hours later, I still had no idea.

Aria was waiting for me by the time I arrived. "There you are!" She waved me over to the machine next to hers. "I've been saving it for you," she explained, tossing her long burgundy ponytail over her shoulder. Even dressed for spin class, she managed to look effortlessly chic. I had never mastered that skill, just as I never had the guts to dye my hair fun colors like she did.

"Hey," I breathed out, giving her a quick hug. "Sorry, I got a little lost in my head after my last meeting." I noticed how she shot a dirty look at a tall, sandy-haired guy on the bike behind mine.

What had I missed? When I arched an eyebrow, silently questioning, she rolled her eyes. Maybe he had wanted the bike she was saving for me.

"A meeting with Noah?" she asked with a giggle. I should've known she'd be aware of the whole drama by now. "How's it looking? Is he completely screwed?"

I smirked, looking her up and down before pulling my hair into a bun. "I'm a little offended that you don't trust my skills."

"Girl, we both know you kick ass at what you do. But come on. This is Noah. He's a goddamn mess." She still managed to sound fond when she said it, but then she could. She didn't know him like I did. No one did. I would have rather swallowed my tongue than tell the girls what happened back then. My brother knew, and he'd been smart enough or at least decent enough to keep it to himself in the years since.

"He'll be fine," I grunted out, arranging my towel and water bottle before climbing onto the bike. "So long as he stays out of my way and doesn't shoot his mouth off to the wrong person."

"It's such bullshit, knowing somebody could just spread lies that easily."

"Well, if he wants to run around with the big boys, he has to face the other side of being a big shot." I caught Aria's confused gaze from the corner of my eye, and it brought me up short. I sounded as angry as I felt. "That's why there are people like me in the world to clean up the messes," I added with a grin I didn't feel.

The energy in the room shifted when Skye entered, her usual blonde hair pulled back in a slicked ponytail. She clapped her hands once to bring all of us to silence. "Are we ready, people? Let's do this!" she called out, overflowing with bright, bubbly excitement we all needed to kickstart our motivation. Despite her willowy frame and platinum blonde hair, a major general couldn't have brought their troops together any more efficiently. If anything, she scared me a little and could definitely kick my ass.

The strangest thought occurred to me as I got comfortable and ready to pedal. There was something close to relief in sitting back and letting somebody else tell me what to do —following the instructor's commands, turning my brain off for a little while—like I had at the club. The way I would've liked to have kept doing if my mystery man hadn't disappeared on me.

It was never far from my thoughts, the memory of how thrilling it was to let him use me. Never had I come like that before. Like my whole body was an instrument, and he was the master.

My legs pumped, and I leaned over the handlebars, gripping them tight, pushing myself through the warm-up. Each leg rotation was a reminder of how sore I was from last night. I had never taken a dick that big, and he hadn't been gentle. What did it say about me that I loved it the way I did? That I craved more?

I could see myself getting hooked on the rush, and that was a dangerous thing.

The idea of living without it now that I knew what I'd been missing out on was enough to make my heart sink with disappointment. But who was I kidding? I had no business thinking about that, anyway.

It had been fun, but I didn't have the first clue as to who exactly had used me. Just the thought of him made my heart flutter, and something told me that had nothing to do with the workout. What a shame I couldn't find my mystery man again since I would be tense like this for as long as I worked with Noah.

I should've asked if I could keep him on retainer. Picturing Noah's face in my head left me gritting my teeth and pedaling faster, completely focused on working my body until I was too exhausted to give a shit about him.

Like I could out-pedal him somehow.

Like I could run away from the shame that still ate me alive whenever I remembered his nasty little smirk and the empty excuses he gave for breaking my heart.

And I was supposed to help him? There wasn't enough money in the world to make me want to do it.

But I *had* to.

And because I had to, I didn't bother waiting until I returned to the office before making a few calls. I had barely caught my breath before I was on the phone, shaking a few trees and calling in a few favors.

The sooner I got Noah out of the public eye, the sooner this would all be over.

8

NOAH

"This is fucking ridiculous." I tapped my fingers against my knee, staring out the limousine window. The city went by in a blur, the streets shining, thanks to rain that had fallen steadily throughout the day.

Putting it mildly, the rain matched my mood. I had spent the day dreading this, knowing I'd have to play nice in front of a bunch of fucking hypocrites. All because the woman sitting on the other side of the back seat told me to put on a tux and be on my best behavior.

"That's right," Sienna muttered, not looking up from the scrolling she was doing on her phone. The gleaming gold case shone in the lights from the traffic around us, one I had never seen. "Get it all out of your system now. I don't want you bitching and moaning during the event."

"Your Wicked Witch impression is getting a little old." However, she was a hell of a lot hotter than a green-faced witch.

Get it together, fuckface. This isn't the time.

"So is your whining," she fired back matter-of-factly.

"And I'd like to remind you, if somebody hated you enough to tear you down, this is all your doing."

My hands flexed, and I realized I was imagining how satisfying it would be to strangle her. I wasn't a violent man. I was a lot of things, but not that. She was determined to make me reconsider.

"We don't have to stay more than an hour or two," she continued in a flat voice. I couldn't understand how she managed to hold a conversation while typing. I had noticed it at her office, and again, I watched her as she spoke. "Make nice, be very grateful to be there, and everything will be fine."

She made it sound easy, but then she could. "So long as I don't have to do any bowing and scraping like some peasant."

"Yeah. God forbid you humble yourself for even five minutes."

"Something's up your ass tonight," I observed. It was much more enjoyable to screw with her than look forward to a night of pretending there was no elephant in the room.

By now, a week after my private life had been upended for the pleasure of gossip hounds across the country, everyone would have read that bullshit excuse for journalism. Yet I knew this world well enough to know I would never be openly scorned by the blue-blood, silver-spoon crowd I was about to face. They would smile at me, give me a few air kisses, and pose for photos like they weren't silently scorning me with every breath. It was all a charade, from top to bottom, and it made me sick.

When Sienna didn't respond, I doubled down. She was the living, breathing symbol of everything I hated about this entire phony setup and the only person in the vicinity for me to take my frustration out on. "If you're going to babysit me, you could at least be decent company," I told her, and in the glow from her screen, I watched her jaw tighten. The sight satisfied me, putting me back on solid ground.

"And if you weren't a baby, you wouldn't need a babysitter." She lowered the phone, narrowing her eyes dangerously from her corner of the seat. She crossed her legs, hidden beneath a long, dark blue silk dress, and began swinging her foot in a way that told me I was in trouble. "I happen to be friends with a few board members, or else I wouldn't have been able to score a last-minute invite for you. It's only right for me to show my face."

"You have a lot of friends, don't you?"

"You say that like it's a bad thing. It is possible to have a wide circle of friends, you know. Not all of us stick solely to the people we grew up with."

"You say that like it's a bad thing," I countered, mimicking her tone. "Last time I checked, you're pretty damn close to the same people we've both known our entire lives."

She blew out a sigh before shaking her head, making her low ponytail shine. "I'm not trying to defend myself to you. You need to be thinking about how much ass you're going to kiss tonight."

She had a way of putting a man in his place. I could give her credit for that much. The only thing that stopped me from hurling an insult was knowing it would only prove her right that I was dreading walking into the lion's den. I would've rather bitten off my tongue than admit it, but the nerves were there—a churning in my gut that left me chugging Pepto to calm things before leaving my penthouse. It didn't matter that those ugly accusations were nothing but lies. What mattered was people would believe them, and the empire I'd built could disappear.

At least Sienna had chosen an event that made sense. A

charity focused on securing housing for low-income families. My real estate career made for a natural tie-in with the foundation's purpose.

We approached the St. Regis Hotel, the site of the gala, and the driver pulled in behind a string of cars unloading their passengers. A cluster of uniformed men held umbrellas at the ready, ushering guests across the sidewalk to keep them dry before they reached the long awning bearing the hotel's name. "Remember," Sienna warned while we pulled up to the front of the line. "Play nice."

It wasn't easy to hold my temper when she insisted on her fucking condescension. "I'm surprised you haven't checked my underwear to make sure I put on a clean pair."

She rolled her eyes, snickering as one of the attendants opened her door. "By the way, you're making a very sizable donation to the foundation."

"Excuse me?" She was already making her graceful exit from the limo, waving to a woman nearby while ducking under the proffered umbrella. I wasted no time getting out of the car, barely acknowledging the guy holding an umbrella for me. "What do you mean, donation?" I demanded of Sienna, trailing a few steps behind her on our way into the hotel.

She released a breathless giggle, running a hand over her slicked-back hair before checking her floor-length dress for damage. I might have taken the opportunity to appreciate how the dress flowed over her tight body if it had belonged to any woman but her.

She was not the woman to ogle unless I craved a kick in the balls. Why couldn't she be ugly, so at least one aspect of this shitfest could be slightly more bearable?

"Would you please calm down?" she asked, her teeth

gritted in a parody of a smile. "What, did you think you were going to get out of this without spending a little cash?"

"I'm already spending a lot of cash," I reminded her in a voice low enough that only she could hear. Countless bodies moved past us in the lobby, but I kept my back to them, ignoring their lighthearted chatter and empty greetings.

"This is not the time to be stingy," she whispered. Her thick lashes fluttered as she stared up at me. "I didn't know you were afraid to drop a few bucks. And here I was, thinking you had all the money you needed at your fingertips."

"I do," I reminded her, grinning at how she rolled her eyes. "I could buy your entire business at a roll of the dice."

"Says you," she muttered.

I ignored it. "I'd like to be consulted before money is spent in my name. Is that too much to ask?"

Those obviously fake lashes fluttered again. Did women think they were fooling anybody? "Forgive me. From now on, you'll be the first to know when I pledge a quarter of a million in your name."

"A quarter—" I forced myself to suck in a breath before my temper exploded. No, I was in no way hurting for the money, but for fuck's sake. I didn't know many people who would take a quarter of a million in their stride when it wasn't their idea to donate the money in the first place.

"This is on me," she murmured. The girl must have missed the memo about her being a terrible actress. Her weak attempt at sorrow left me wishing I'd brought Pepto along. "I'll run that sort of thing by you next time. I promise."

"You could try not looking quite so proud of yourself when you apologize."

Light danced in her blue eyes before she nodded. "I'll keep that in mind." I was being hustled, plain and simple, something I had to live with as we walked side-by-side across the lobby, following the flow of traffic into the ballroom.

I didn't have time to stop before bumping against the arm, which Sienna threw out to the side to halt my progress. "Photographers. Give them your prettiest smile, now," she murmured while I did exactly that. Evidently, it wasn't enough because she added, "Try to make it look like you're not on your way to the guillotine. Try to think of something that makes you smile for real."

Of all times for my pink-haired mystery woman to come to mind. Fuck, she was good, so good I had jerked off to the memory more than once in the days since our encounter. It had been so gratifying, knowing she was nervous and apprehensive, but breaking down her walls just the same. It was the sort of rush nothing else could deliver. There wasn't a deal in existence that had ever or could ever bring me that level of satisfaction.

"I would ask what you were thinking about just then..." Sienna whispered once the photographer moved on. "But I'm afraid of what I would hear."

"It's nothing for your innocent ears," I confirmed, but I couldn't pretend not to notice her scowl as we stepped into the busy ballroom. "Smile, or people might think you don't love your job."

Because if she acted like a raging bitch with a stick wedged up her ass, I could make her regret it.

"Is that Noah Goldsmith?" I turned to the sound of my name being called and groaned softly when I recognized Mabel Curtis, who was roughly a hundred years old and wore enough cloying perfume that my head spun. "I thought that was you! You look so much like your father, Ari, it's difficult to tell you apart."

She was a longtime, faithful Farrah Goldsmith client, and as such, I had a responsibility to be friendly even as my nostrils burned. Why did old women always have to wear the same perfume? And why did they bathe in it?

She shook her head and clicked her tongue before continuing her monologue. "I was so sorry to hear about all this mess in the press. Trust me, nobody believes it."

I had heard some lies in my life, but this had to take the cake. "I appreciate your support," I managed to murmur through clenched teeth. "Forgive my manners. Do you know Sienna Black?"

Thank fuck. She turned to Sienna, smiling wide enough to show off the lipstick on her teeth. "Of course! Sienna's mother decorated my Sag Harbor house."

I left the two of them to chat pleasantly for a few moments, scanning the ballroom over the top of their heads. What a surprise, the number of people whose gaze darted away from mine as soon as I looked their way. Hypocrites, every last one of them.

Once Sienna was free, I leaned down to mutter in her ear. "How many of the men in this room have paid off a nanny after fucking her during naptime?"

"That's none of our business," she reminded me in a light, almost playful tone, looking around before wiggling her fingers in a wave to a passing couple. "And that's not what we're here for."

"Fucking hypocrites need to look in a mirror," I muttered. My tie was too tight, cutting off my air, and I hooked a finger beneath my collar in a vain attempt at finding a little comfort.

"Would you stop fidgeting?" she snapped in a whisper,

handing me a glass of champagne as we wound through the clusters of people dotting the spacious room. "You are the generous benefactor tonight, remember? We don't need any photos of you scowling like a toddler who missed naptime. Now, let's check out the silent auction." Tucking her hand inside my elbow, she tugged gently in the direction of an elaborate display set up on the far side of the room.

"What, I haven't given them enough money tonight?" It still stuck in my craw, the fact that she hadn't thought to check in with me before making a pledge like that. Was it not bad enough I was watching my life slip away, losing a little more control all the time?

"Look who it is." Before we could reach the auction tables, a familiar and unwelcome presence made itself known in the form of Drake Thomas, who sauntered our way, holding a glass of champagne and wearing a shit-eating grin that could only mean one thing. He was looking to start something. "I hate to tell you, but I already took a look at what was up for auction. There are no Get Out of Jail Free cards available. But then, you're not in jail, are you? Not literally."

"Sorry," I countered, accepting his handshake even as my skin crawled at having to make contact with the snake who'd gone out of his way to undermine me for years. Jealous that I'd built a business twice as large in half the time it took him to build Thomas Properties. I was younger and smarter, and it killed him. "Maybe I'm not too quick on the uptake this evening. Was that supposed to be a joke?"

He nodded slowly. "Understandable. With everything you're going through right now, you must be beside yourself. Your thoughts have to be racing in a million different directions. Truly, I was sorry to read all those ugly allegations last week. It must have come as a real shock."

For all I knew, this bastard had been the one to set the match to the fuse and blow the whole thing up. "Oh, you know how it is," I replied with an easy shrug. "There are so many jealous, petty people out there, willing to say and do anything to undermine the competition when they know they don't have a prayer of beating them honestly."

"How are you?" Sienna asked in an overly bright voice, sliding her body between his and mine. "It's nice to see you here. What do you think? Is it worth me putting a bid down on anything over there?" She jerked her chin in the direction of the table, where countless guests laughed and joked about who would come out on top when it came time to announce the winning bids. Because to them, this was all fun. A game. Their futures weren't in jeopardy, no matter how much worse their sins were than mine.

Fuck, how I hated them for it.

But not as much as I hated how Drake looked Sienna up and down. The prick barely managed not to lick his thin lips. "Tell me you're not here with Noah Goldsmith," he said with a groan before chuckling like we were all friends. "I could show you a *much* better time."

If he thought that would get under my skin, he was wasting his time. That didn't stop me from placing a hand on her waist and stepping up a little closer. "If I didn't know better, I would think you're trying to poach my date. There I was, thinking you only poached other people's clients."

"I don't need to do any poaching," he muttered while his gaze went steely. "There's plenty of them lying around, just waiting to be snapped up. As it turns out, people don't like doing business with shady characters. They would much rather go with somebody they know they can trust."

"And as long as you can fool them into trusting you, you may as well take advantage," I agreed.

"It was very nice to see you." Sienna closed her hand over mine, squeezing hard enough to grind my bones before she pulled me along with her, away from him. We weren't able to move ten feet before being stopped again.

"Oh, Noah!" I vaguely recognized the old man who placed himself in our path. "The man of the hour! We would love it if you would say a few words." Right. Chairman of the foundation and a general pain in the ass who loved to hear himself speak. I couldn't remember his name, but who gave a shit when I was a deer caught in headlights?

"A few words." My brain threatened to shut down thanks to overwhelm. I felt Drake's eyes bore holes into the back of my head while the old man smiled expectantly at me.

Sienna laughed lightly. "What an honor," she announced. "But come on now, Benjamin. You know better than to put somebody on the spot like this. You're such a rascal."

The worst part was he fucking loved it. The man ate it up with a spoon. It's probably the only time a beautiful woman had ever teased him.

"All right, but the opportunity is there," he insisted, barely able to pry his eyes from her long enough to glance at me. "I'm sure everyone here is sick to death of hearing me speak."

It was all too much. There was a reason I didn't bother with shit like this. Let me hold court in a busy club, surrounded by fawning women? I was in my element. I could talk for hours, for days. Ask me to get up in front of several hundred people who hadn't stopped watching my every move since I walked through the door. An entirely different story.

"I'm over this," I murmured in Sienna's ear once

Benjamin was pulled away by an old crone, probably his wife. The blistering look she gave Sienna confirmed that as if Sienna gave a damn about her husband.

She turned to me, scowling. "Are you serious? We haven't been here thirty minutes. They haven't even served dinner, and you want to run away?"

I didn't know whether she said it to goad me. I only knew it was for the best that I got the hell out of that room before I blew up and took hundreds of people with me. On my way out, I somehow managed not to plow through the crowd and send people flying like bowling pins. Bolting down what was left of my champagne, I handed the empty flute to a server before retreating to the lobby.

"Where are you going?" Sienna's heels tapped against the floor behind me, her voice like a snake's hiss. That was what she was. A fucking snake, like Drake Thomas and half the people in that ballroom. Soothing their guilty consciences, at least I didn't pretend to give a shit about the underprivileged while comparing the square footage of their vacation homes.

"Where do you think I'm going? Anywhere but here." She let out a strangled, panicked sound, but she didn't need to bother. There was nobody around to hear, most of the guests having retreated inside to drink, sip subpar champagne, and pat themselves on the back for being such wonderful, caring citizens.

The rain had turned to a light mist that swirled through the air by the time I made it outside beneath the protection of the awning. The air was cool and crisp and went a long way toward easing the burning sensation in my chest. I wasn't exactly calm when Sienna grabbed my arm, but I could breathe more freely. There was no longer the sense of an overturned hive of bees buzzing around inside my skull.

"Excuse me, but I had to kiss a lot of ass to get a last-minute invite tonight," she grunted out, her face flushed, teeth bared. "And you haven't spent nearly enough time showing your face."

"Haven't you heard? I'm the man of the hour. I'm dumping a shit ton of money into the foundation."

"That's not enough. Why don't you get that?" she demanded. "I thought you wanted to turn all this around and salvage your reputation. The first challenge you come up against, you fold."

"You know what? I'm beginning to regret ever calling you." She stared at me, incredulous. "I mean it. Let's stop pretending this is about doing your job and call it what it really is."

Her head snapped back like she was honestly surprised, which I could not believe. "Illuminate me. What is this really about, Noah?"

"It's about you having me where you want me... under your thumb. Don't pretend you're not getting off on this," I insisted when she scoffed. "I see straight through you. You love watching me squirm."

"You really, and I mean this, *need* to get over yourself." But I wasn't fooled. I saw the way she blushed. I heard the tremor in her voice.

"You can manage this with no help from me," I decided. "Hand over my hard-earned money to whoever the hell you think would look best in the press. But I'll be damned if I let you parade me around like a fucking dog on a leash."

I was halfway to the curb when her voice rang out behind me. "I hope you and your ego are happy together because that's all you're going to have to your name."

I tuned her out, hailing a cab at random. I couldn't remember the last time I got into a cab, but it mattered more to be away from those judgmental fucks as quickly as I could. I wasn't running away, no matter what Sienna thought. This was self-preservation.

Yet somehow, though I knew damn well it was smart to take myself out of the equation before I made a bad situation infinitely worse, it wasn't enough to believe I was making the right choice. I wanted her to believe it too.

There was nothing to do but sit with that frustration through the drive home, wondering how long it would take to burn a hole through me.

9

SIENNA

"**D**o yourself a favor and at least try to relax." I checked my phone to be sure the reporter hadn't sent a message saying she was running late while Noah paced like a restless animal, crossing his SoHo penthouse living room for approximately the hundredth time since I'd arrived early for his interview.

"It had better not be a hit job," he warned in a growl while adjusting his large, flashy, probably worth-a-mint watch. He was pulling out all the stops today to look impressive.

"Am I supposed to be intimidated right now?" I asked with a sigh. "Because really, you should be practicing what you're going to say."

"Why do I need to practice when you already have a list of talking points for me?" he retorted. This again. He'd been complaining about my preparation for the past two days since I sent the questions and answers over to him.

"If I didn't know better, I would think you're not grateful for all the work I'm putting into this," I said with a sigh. "For what it's worth, this is a play from the same playbook I've used a thousand times. It works."

"I'm not a child. I can speak for myself." He turned to face me, his hands on his slim hips. With the light from floor-to-ceiling windows hitting him from behind, he made a pretty impressive picture. I had to remind myself not to stare at his body for too long, the way I'd avoid staring at the sun for fear of getting burned. His crisp, white button-down was open at the collar, making him look roguishly sexy.

Why did he have to be so damn sexy?

More importantly, why did I have to notice?

It didn't help that we'd spent more time alone since the article was published than we had in the past ten years combined. Until now, I'd been able to avoid him. The force of his magnetism had no chance to affect me. But there was a flip side to that. I had no means of resisting him. I hadn't been able to build up a tolerance to the potent combination of looks, body, and confidence that was damn near enough to rock me back on my heels, and that was while he insisted on acting like a spoiled little bitch. Maybe it was better for him to keep whining, or else I might've had no choice but to jump him to get it out of my system.

"Remember, this is what I do." It was safer for me to switch into professional mode, babying my client like I'd babied so many others. "This is all about making things as easy for you as possible. I've already gotten some positive feedback after your appearance at the fundraiser."

"Give me a fucking break," he growled out, running a hand through his dark hair and sighing like a man with the weight of the world on his shoulders. "Your people planted all that positive shit online."

"Of course, that's how it's done," I sighed. "But there have been positive comments made from people outside my company. The social media team for the foundation reposted photos of you and couldn't have kissed your ass any harder. This is positive progress."

His head dropped back so he could bark a bitter laugh at the ceiling high above our heads. "They kissed my ass because I gave them a lot of money."

"I never took you as naïve." Something about the way I said it cut off his snide laughter. "What, you don't think that's the way it works? Money erases a lot of sins."

He checked his watch again, frowning even though we had a few minutes before our scheduled time. "Well, hell, I could've done this on my own if that was all it took."

"You know, you are more than free to get rid of me if that's what you really want." I met his hard stare without blinking, without so much as flinching, while he tried to stare holes through me. "By all means. See how far you can get on your own. I really wish you would try."

It would mean going back to normal—avoiding him, pretending he was a bug under my shoe and not a ridiculously hot man with a dangerous effect on my lady parts all of a sudden.

"And deprive you of the pleasure of making a horse's ass out of me?" He arched an eyebrow, a smirk beginning to stir.

"Oh, Noah. You're doing an excellent job of that on your own." I had the pleasure of hearing the growl he couldn't hold back before the intercom buzzed. That sound felt oddly familiar, like an echo from the past. He crossed the room in a handful of long strides and pressed his finger to the speaker button. "Yes?" he barked out, making me cringe. It probably was not the best idea to get into an argument with a reporter on the way, but he had a way of making me forget what I knew to be true.

One of us had to be the bigger person, and it would have to be me.

"You have a Gretchen Harris down here to see you, sir," the front desk manager reported.

"Send her up." With his back to me, his shoulders rose and fell. "This had better not turn into a disaster," he muttered.

"That's up to you," I reminded him, more gently this time. He needed to cool off before Gretchen arrived, and the elevator was awfully fast. "I've given you everything you need to make this a success. Trust me, okay? I do know what I'm talking about."

"So long as it's over fast. I still have a company to run." He shook his hands and rolled his head from side to side. "And you say you're friends with this girl?"

"We've worked together before." I looked him over, admitting to myself, if not to him, that he looked damn good in his perfectly tailored navy suit. "Don't worry about that. You are Noah-fucking-Goldsmith. You've got this. It's time to have your side of the story heard."

His brows drew together when he looked my way. "If I didn't know better, I would think you meant that."

"I do." *I didn't.* I had spoken those words to more people than I could possibly remember. Countless clients who had ended up appreciating my expertise. I could rattle them off the way I rattled off my own name. "Gretchen will do right by you. I trust her."

As if on cue, she knocked on the door. I made it a point to answer, greeting her with a hug and kiss on her cheek. Before releasing her, I whispered, "Go easy on him. He's got an ego the size of his penthouse." She laughed softly, nodding in understanding when she pulled back.

I wasn't more than three strides from the door when I

realized this was a mistake. It wasn't that I lacked faith in Gretchen. Not even close. She was the best, a pro at wording a story so it came off well-balanced and fair, even if it was nothing but a carefully orchestrated fluff piece, the way it would be today.

The petite, adorable Gretchen wasn't the problem. On the other hand, the six-foot-three tower of hormones was currently sizing her up? My heart sank when I caught the whiff of desire in the air, but I forced my way through it rather than slapping him upside the head. I couldn't have reached it if I tried not unless I jumped. "Noah Goldsmith, meet Gretchen Harris."

"Gretchen. Such a pleasure." *Oh, this pitiful jackass.* A sour taste flooded my mouth as he engulfed her outstretched hand with both of his, his voice deeper and warmer than anything I'd heard so far. "I'm sure you must be busy. I can't tell you how much I appreciate you taking the time to sit down with me today."

Would it come off the wrong way if I burst out laughing? I decided not to take the chance, ushering Gretchen to the leather sofa positioned opposite a flatscreen television that was more like a movie screen. "Would you like anything to drink?" I asked her, eyeing Noah warily as he sank to the other end of the sofa, his body angled toward hers.

Please, do not screw this up. I made it a point to seek his gaze and hold it as I perched on a chair, glaring at him while Gretchen was getting settled in. His lips stirred in the beginnings of an arrogant grin, and something told me I was fucked.

She tucked a strand of strawberry-blonde hair behind her ear, clearing her throat before tapping her phone and setting it between them. "Okay, Mr. Goldsmith, I'm going to record this if you don't mind, so I can go back and review things. It's a lot easier to be accurate if I have a recording to go from."

"By all means." He stretched one long arm across the back of the sofa, the picture of casual grace as if he hadn't finished pacing around like a nervous child only moments before she arrived, complaining about his precious time being wasted. "I'm sure you know what you're doing."

She might not have heard the meaning behind his words, but I sure as hell did. He didn't bother hiding it. Either she wasn't picking up on it, or she was too much of a professional to let it show. The girl was no idiot, that much was for sure, and I doubted she was a stranger to being hit on by random men. Why did men always think they were the first to invent flirting?

"Mr. Goldsmith, tell me..." Turning his way, she offered a warm smile. "What made you decide to strike out on your own when you could have taken a leadership position in your family's company?"

He lifted a broad shoulder, chuckling. "Where is the fun in that?"

I would kill him. I would absolutely fucking kill him. That was not the response he was supposed to offer. I cleared my throat so loudly he couldn't pretend he hadn't heard me. As soon as our eyes met, I shook my head. *Do not screw this up.*

He chuckled softly, shrugging again. "At the end of the day, what I wanted more than an easy position was something I could call my own. I was inspired by my great-grandmother's legacy, not to mention my mother, Olivia, both strong women and entrepreneurs. They showed me what it meant to build something lasting. I'm forever indebted to them for that."

Thank God. I released some of the breath I was holding

but was not exactly relaxed. We still had a long way to go before we were out of the woods.

"What made you choose real estate?" she asked, and he rattled off the prepared response. Another relief, enough to let me lower my shoulders from up around my ears.

Before she could ask another question, Noah leaned closer. I watched, holding my breath, while he squinted. "Sorry, but I can't help noticing your earrings. They're very pretty."

"Oh, thank you." She touched her hand to the pearls dangling in a teardrop setting from both ears. "They belonged to my grandmother."

"No offense to your grandmother, but I can't imagine them looking any better on her than they do on you." They shared a quiet laugh while bile rushed into my throat. It wasn't so much the fact that he insisted on flirting, even if his compulsion sickened me.

She was into it. Her soft giggles, the way she bit her lip after breaking eye contact. I wasn't blind. I'd watched more than one woman melt under the charm of this man, and she was no different.

"I'm going to grab a bottle of water," I announced much too loudly. What the hell did I care? He was determined to turn this into something it wasn't supposed to be, and she was all too happy to follow along. It was enough to make me consider something much stronger than water.

On my way past Noah, I leaned down to whisper in his ear. "Remember how you ended up in this position," I warned, continuing to the kitchen.

It was an open floor plan, so there was no hiding my growing irritation. I could only turn to face the refrigerator, grab a bottle, and take a deep gulp of the icy cold liquid. It was a startling contrast to the heat threatening to burn me alive.

Where the hell did he get off? What was wrong with his brain? Of all times for him to resist his nature, yet all he could do was salivate over a pretty girl.

Maybe it was better for me to keep my distance. I lingered in the kitchen, my back against the quartz counter-top, sipping water as they went back and forth. "I'll have to keep you in mind if I ever look for a new place," she promised, laughing softly before tucking her hair behind her ear again. "Though I don't think I could afford the sort of properties you specialize in."

I turned to watch as Noah pursed his lips thoughtfully. "You never know," he drawled with a grin, even I could admit would melt my panties if he turned it my way. "I've been known to make a good deal in my time. I might be able to help you find something for a steal."

Was it my imagination, or had he inched closer to her side of the couch? What made it so much worse was how she now mirrored his body language—leaning toward him, her legs crossed in his direction. Every filthy thought running through his head was written plainly on his face. It was enough to make me wonder if I should leave them alone.

My stomach sank like a rock. Sure, it seemed like things were going well, but for how long? He couldn't possibly keep this going without finally saying something hopelessly stupid or worthy of a sexual harassment accusation.

Only if she considers it harassment and not an invitation at this rate.

I set my water down on the counter, and the sound was loud enough to pull Gretchen's focus back to the interview. She sat up straight, looking down at her notes, clearly flustered. "I understand you recently made a large donation to a foundation devoted to providing quality housing to low-income and disadvantaged families. Can you tell me more about that?"

He easily launched into his prepared statement, adding enough of a personal flourish that a stranger might think he meant every word of it. Well, I couldn't get on his case for that. He was doing what I had asked him to do.

But I had not asked him to flirt shamelessly. I should have known better than to think he was capable of forgetting about his dick for even an hour.

At the end of the hour, Gretchen offered a regretful little sigh and ended the recording. "This is going to make a terrific article," she assured him as she stood, smoothing out invisible wrinkles in her tight skirt. And, of course, what was he doing? Watching her. It would be a miracle if I did not kill him before this was over. I started to think Jules had been right all along that this was a bad idea. It had been fun at first, imagining how he would squirm, but it wasn't worth putting myself through the grief of watching him undermine what I had put in place.

I went through the motions of promising to follow up with Gretchen and even entertained the idea of getting together for brunch soon—at least, I pretended to. The sooner she was out of the penthouse, the better. I didn't need a member of the press witnessing me tearing Noah's head from his neck.

"Well..." He sounded surprisingly lighthearted when he turned my way, grinning from ear to ear once Gretchen left. "I have to admit, that wasn't so bad. You didn't tell me she was hot."

Wrong move.

So very wrong.

"And in what world does that make a damn bit of difference?" I snapped, throwing my hands into the air. "Goddamn you and your libido."

"Grow up," he chortled. "You know what I meant. It was easy to talk to her. You could take lessons."

The man was determined to say the exact wrong thing. "You must have a death wish," I muttered, shaking my head. "It's the only explanation that makes any sense."

"Come on." He waved a dismissive hand. "Lighten up. That's all I was trying to say."

His attitude set my teeth on edge. If this kept up much longer, I'd commit my first murder. "Let's call it what it really was." My heels clicked against the floor as I followed him through the living room while he walked around, grabbing his keys and phone. "You were hitting on her, and she was too busy giggling and blushing to remember she was here to do a job."

"Try not to sound so jealous." He shot me a snide look over his shoulder, telling me he had no idea how close he was coming to his last breath. "Admit it. The interview went even better than you imagined, and you're pissy over me getting along with a hot girl."

No. That wasn't it at all. *Was it?* Resentment threatened to choke me by the time I found my voice again. "So if she had been unattractive, you would have clammed up? Is that what you're saying? This entire thing rode on whether or not you could imagine fucking her?"

"Give me a break!" Of course, he had to play dumb as he turned my way, rolling his eyes and sighing like he was a victim. "Could you take the stick out of your ass for a minute? Why does everything have to be a fucking fight with you?"

"Why does everything have to be an opportunity for you

to get your dick wet?" Was I screaming? Not exactly, but I was damn close. It was either that or hit him at this point. "What is it going to take for you to understand? You ended up where you are now because of shit like what you said to Gretchen during that interview. 'I could get a deal for you,' " I quoted, deepening my voice and puffing out my chest. "Maybe you can come sit on my lap, and we'll discuss specifics."

"I didn't say that," he growled out, lowering his brow before he began to slowly advance. I didn't like the light in his eyes. There was something dangerous in them. Foreboding.

Holding up my chin, I laughed bitterly. "You didn't have to! It was obvious that was what you meant!"

"It wasn't." He blinked rapidly, scowling while searching my face. "I'm serious. That was not what I meant."

"You could have fucking fooled me, Noah. There is your problem in a nutshell. You don't stop to think about how people might take the things you say, which is why all the PR in the world isn't going to help you. This is a mistake." The words fell from my lips before I knew what I was saying. By the time I realized what I'd said, it was too late. I had to follow through.

And it wasn't like I was wrong—quite the opposite. There was no hope of helping him if it meant witnessing his casual, careless attitude and arrogance toward women. I thought I hated him before this. It turned out I had barely scratched the surface of what was possible.

"Where the hell do you think you're going?" he demanded when I turned, marching toward the door.

"Figure it out," I snapped. To hell with this. It was a mistake from the beginning. "I am not going to sit around and watch you sabotage yourself. Manage this on your own because I can't help you."

"Are you serious?" Damn that long stride of his. He made it to the door a split second before I did, slamming his hand against the surface, making it impossible for me to pull it open. Leaning over me, he growled out, "We have an agreement, you and I. You don't get to walk away."

"Read the contract," I suggested, turning around with a sigh that I hoped would cover up how nervous he made me, being so close. The intensity behind his stony glare lifted the hair on my neck. "You'll find I *can* do this. You've only paid me a nonrefundable deposit, and either party is free to walk away at any time. Or does the big, bad businessman not bother reading contracts before he signs them?"

He snorted, shaking his head. "I didn't know you were a quitter."

A laugh bubbled out of me before I knew it was coming. "Please. Are we children? You think it's that easy to goad me into doing this?"

Looking me up and down, he snickered, shaking his head. "Call it what you want, but I know a quitter when I see one."

"And I know a stupid, scared little boy when I see one." He didn't want me to leave? That was fine. Then he would have to hear what was on my mind. "You're too scared to sit through an interview without falling back on what you do best... trying to charm and seduce your way out of it."

"Is that so?" Instead of backing off, he leaned in until I was trapped between him and the door. Dear God, he was overwhelming. "Tell me more about myself," he murmured in a deceptively soft voice. I felt his breath on my face and shivered, then hoped like hell he didn't notice. My body didn't know what to do any more than my overheated brain did.

One thing I was sure of. No way was I going to back down now. Not even when his nearness left my knees trembling and my heart fluttering like a hummingbird's wings. "You can't help yourself even when the fucking answers are handed to you. All you had to do was play along, but you couldn't. I can't trust you. I don't work with people I can't trust to act like adults."

His head bobbed slowly while a snide smirk twisted his generous mouth. "Right. Keep telling yourself that's why you're too chickenshit to see this through. Or too bitter." At least he backed off, allowing me to breathe. It was easier to keep a grip on myself when I wasn't battling the tantalizing scent of his spicy cologne.

Yet another reason why this was a doomed arrangement. "Good luck clawing your way out of the hole you dug." I yanked the door open before he could stop me and walked out without looking back.

I had never quit anything in my life, but there was a first time for everything. At that point, it was either walking away and absorbing the blowback or sticking around and associating myself with what would inevitably come crashing down.

All the while, wondering why I had never wanted to kill him more than I had when I saw him smile at Gretchen.

10

NOAH

"I have to say, the numbers look good. Much along the lines of what we discussed weeks back." Arthur Pine glanced across the table toward his brother, Jim, who nodded his agreement. A pair of ridiculously wealthy, middle-aged tech gurus looking to diversify their investment portfolio and branch out into real estate. "And you've secured a development partnership with ZF Construction?"

Working with the Barrett Black construction company sweetened the pot, no doubt. I told myself they were more interested in his name than in the idea of him legitimizing the deal. I didn't have to worry about the article. Things were looking up—no more phone calls or texts from members of the press, nobody waiting for me outside my apartment building in hopes of getting a picture or a quote they could use.

"Yes, Mr. Black is eager to collaborate with us on developing the parcel once the sale has been secured." We were looking to develop a piece of land on the north shore of Long Island, the idea being to build a townhome development along with an adjoining upscale shopping center and dining for the convenience of the residents.

"We'll take these final figures back to our team, but from what I see here, I'm satisfied." Jim finished what was left of his coffee, then dabbed the corners of his mouth with a napkin. "We hate to run like this, but we have a meeting across town at the top of the hour. You understand."

"Of course." Standing, I shook their hands, assuring them I would cover our brunch bill. Considering this was my first major win in weeks, I would've covered just about anything. We made plans to connect by the end of the week, and I looked forward to sharing the news with Maxim once I reached the office. He needed a win too.

What a shame I couldn't tell my PR manager about it and thank her for the work, which must have contributed to the deal advancing. Two weeks ago, the Pine brothers were practically ducking my calls, playing phone tag with me. Rather, their assistant was, since I couldn't get them on the phone. After the donation to the housing foundation and the goodwill that had been stirred up after that, along with my unequivocal denial of the charges in that bullshit article, it seemed I had regained a little trust.

It was then that I checked my emails. One came through from Momentum Public Relations, Sienna's PR company, but it wasn't from her.

I scanned it, some bullshit next-level instructions from someone I'd never heard of. It made my blood boil. Had she seriously ghosted me completely and washed her hands of me?

When I wanted to speak to Sienna about my morning win, I get this? She'd been MIA since the interview at my place, and part of me was relieved she'd left when she did. But another part of me, the part that couldn't shake her from my mind, wished she hadn't gone. It was a dangerous game, being near her. She was like a flame, drawing me in despite the risk of getting burned. Her absence only intensified my desire, making it hard to keep myself away from thoughts of her. Like it or not, she was pretty damn irresistible. I was only a man, flesh and blood, so it wasn't surprising for a beautiful woman to affect me.

I did not, however, take well to being ignored. The email made me change my plans out of nowhere, walking to her office rather than heading back to my own. She couldn't avoid me if I were in her face.

However, as it turned out, I wasn't in her face when I arrived at her sleek headquarters, where a dozen employees tapped rapidly on their keyboards as I stepped off the elevator. Blowing past the receptionist, I strode smoothly toward the opposite corner of the floor.

Sienna's assistant spotted me and almost jumped out of her chair before I reached her. "I'm sorry, Miss Black is at a meeting in Midtown. She has another appointment after that, and she was going to let me know if she'd come back to the office afterward or if she would finish out the day at home."

I thanked her assistant, whose name I still didn't know and didn't care to, before asking, "What about her partner? Jules something? Is she around?"

"My ears are burning." I turned at the voice over my shoulder and found myself face-to-face with a petite, curly-headed blonde. Normally, a person had to know me before looking at me with so much wry uneasiness etched on their face. Considering we have never met, I had to assume Sienna told her about me.

"Jules Sherman." She extended a hand, offering a firm shake. "I guess she didn't tell you."

"Tell me what?"

"She's left the work in the capable hands of our senior staff." She was quick to tell me while I tried to process the news. "If I understand correctly, she's handling the setup for the sports clinic on her own, as it's a bit more complicated to work out the scheduling. You'll be posing for photos with star athletes and smiling kids within the next couple of weeks, though, rest assured. Was there something you wanted to discuss?"

So this was how it would be, getting the brush-off. She didn't have the balls to tell me to go fuck myself. Then again, she had told me in her own way by walking out on me after the interview. Only, I'd figured she was bluffing.

Nobody walked away from me.

"Jules?" A girl on the other side of the floor called out, waving an arm over her head. "Your eleven-thirty call."

"That's right. Be there in a second." Jules offered a tight, professional smile. "Don't worry. Everything's looking up. We've got plenty of goodwill flowing your way."

I'd had the same thought on the way over, but it wasn't enough. Standing alone in the middle of a hallway, surrounded by young women at tastefully decorated desks, it was then I realized all of the employees were female and may as well have been alone.

How could she leave me floundering like this? Was I supposed to accept this bullshit at face value? She didn't know me at all if she thought I would accept her ghosting me without explanation.

A switch flipped in my head, and when I turned back toward Sienna's assistant's desk, I had a plan in place. "Excuse me," I offered, wearing my most charming smile as I approached her like a man without a care in the world. "Any chance you can tell me where I'd find Sienna?"

She peered up at me over the rims of her glasses.
"Excuse me?"

"Miss Black. You said she was at a meeting. She left
something at my apartment during the interview with
Gretchen Harris on Monday. I've been wanting to get it back
to her."

"You could leave it here," she offered, nodding toward
Sienna's office door.

"I would rather hand it directly to her if it's all the same.
It's been weighing on my conscience for days." Winking, I
added, "I've already been accused of being no good, filthy
scum. I don't want to add thief to the list."

I knew her smile. I had seen it so many times on the
faces of so many women. She knew she should resist but
couldn't find it in her to do so. "Okay," she whispered,
tapping on her keyboard. "Don't tell her you found out
from me."

"I would never," I assured her.

The restaurant was bustling with the early lunch crowd
when I arrived.

"Can I help you, sir?"

I barely noticed the voice of the chipper girl at the
hostess stand while scanning the dining room, searching for
a familiar brunette. "I'm looking for someone having lunch
here," I explained without looking her way.

Sunlight gleamed off rich, dark brown hair by the
window, looking out over Park Avenue. Across from her sat a
vaguely familiar man—an actor in town from Hollywood,
working on a new play, if memory served. The closer I got,

the less I liked how he was looking at her. And the way she smiled at him.

Everything in the room went red, my head pounding harder with each step. They looked a hell of a lot more like a date than a business meeting. Whatever it was they wanted to call it was about to come to an end once I arrived at their table.

"Sienna. And there I was, thinking you dropped off the face of the earth." I took a second to enjoy her flustered surprise—mouth falling open, eyes going wide before her gaze darted toward the douchebag sitting across from her.

"Noah Goldsmith, what a surprise. Have you met Jacob Dalton?" She recovered quickly. Ever the professional.

"No, I haven't had the pleasure." And I wasn't looking to have it, either. Rather than acknowledge him, I maintained focus on her. "There's something we need to discuss."

Her brittle smile threatened to shatter her teeth. "I'm busy at the moment."

"Get unbusy," I muttered.

"Yo, do you need a minute?" Jacob asked.

Sienna and I were locked in a staring contest. She blinked first, something murderous washing over her face before she nodded. "Yes, I need to step outside for a minute. Sorry about this," she told him, and the sight of her simpering smile felt like a knife to the chest.

Why? I wasn't sure where it came from. Probably the fact that I'd spent days on her pay-no-mind list, only to find her flirting with this asshole.

She managed to wait until we were outside before whirling on me, folding her arms over a painfully hip jeans-and-tee outfit, very much unlike the suits she wore when we met. It was as if she wore a costume depending on the sort of client she was handling. "I am not going to do what I want to do right now," she gritted out, glaring at me. "Because we don't need any negative press, and dozens of people inside the restaurant could look out and see us. But please, don't take that to mean I don't want to kill you right now because I would like nothing more. What goes on in your head? How *dare* you?"

"It's my fault you pushed me to this point?" When she scoffed, it was my turn to grind my teeth. "For days, you've been ducking me. I want an explanation."

"And I want a house in the Maldives, but that doesn't mean I'll snap my fingers and get it. Things are moving fine. I am not going to hold your hand every second of the day. If that's what you want, find yourself a babysitter."

I barely heard her over my pounding heart. "And *then!* I find you sucking up to some skinny jean-wearing asshole with a man bun."

"That asshole happens to be a client," she hissed. The look she shot toward the windows made me roll my eyes. He couldn't hear us out here.

"Do you flirt with all of your clients?"

"Do you?" she fired back. Of all times for my dick to wake up and pay attention. It had to be the anger and the energy being created. Otherwise, this was the least likely time for me to get a hard-on. She tossed her head, sending a wave of scent my way, distracting me from why I was there.

Her hair smelled like vanilla and some flower I couldn't identify. I would gladly have buried my nose in those luscious waves to drink in the smell.

"Well?" She prompted, and I realized I'd been drifting off.

Nope. Definitely not the time to get confused by sweet-smelling hair. I clenched my jaw before growling out, "You will not ignore me from now on. Understood?"

"And you will not tell me what to do, nor will you tell me how to run my business. Understood?" She tossed her hair again when a gust of wind stirred it, making me groan softly. "I'm doing the work I'm contracted to do. Your article is coming out tomorrow, and it's a goddamn love letter. What else do you want, Noah?"

My mouth opened and closed. What was it about the question that made it impossible to think? I want your attention. No, that didn't sound right. What did I want? "I want my messages acknowledged, at the very least. I am not the man you ghost. Get it?"

"I'm trembling," she deadpanned.

My fists clenched when a wave of rage tried to knock me on my ass. "Fuck off."

"Is that any way to talk to me when I'm saving your ass?" With a withering look, she breezed past me on her way inside the restaurant. "Now, excuse me, I have another client whose hand needs to be held at the moment. If you want to talk to me, make an appointment."

The only thing that kept my temper in check was knowing I was out on the street. I couldn't have all of Park Avenue witnessing me throwing a fit. I doubted even someone with Sienna's connections could help me out of a disaster like that.

My feet pounded the pavement while a burning sensation spread through my chest. Something about the way I walked or the look on my face made a pair of women step aside, almost flinching away from me. I must have looked like I was ready to commit murder, which wasn't far from the way I felt.

Why did she have to be so fucking impossible? Why couldn't she meet me halfway? Everything had to be a goddamn fight.

It would be different if she fell for my charm.

And that was the problem. Block after block, I walked, turning it over in my mind. I couldn't charm her. It was impossible. She hated me too much to bend an inch, and I wasn't used to that. I didn't know how to deal with a woman I couldn't work around. Hell, even my mother was a sucker when I turned on the charm.

But not Sienna.

I couldn't let it go more than I could let go of wanting her approval for some unknown reason. Another first, giving a shit what anybody thought of me, man or woman.

I was no closer to calming down when I reached my office, where I once again parted crowds and silenced chatter simply by walking down the hall. I caught more than one worried look on my way to the solitude of my office.

How was I supposed to get anything done when the only thing on my mind was tracking down that actor and using that man bun of his to slam his face into a table?

I needed a release. I needed to forget everything for a little while.

I needed a night at Dante's club. Whether or not the pink-haired woman was there didn't matter. I would find some willing body to take out my frustrations come hell or high water.

11

SIENNA

"I am so sorry about that." I smiled as I took my seat across from Jacob, but inside was a different story.

How? How did he always do it to me? I told myself to be the adult, to have the cooler head, yet there I was, flustered and furious, not to mention feeling like a smacked ass thanks to the little scene Noah had caused.

Jacob waved it off. "Nah, don't worry about it. I guess you have a lot of people who want a piece of your time."

"Something like that." The salad I was enjoying the hell out of only a few minutes ago didn't look so appetizing anymore. Was there anything Noah couldn't ruin? "Did those couple of minutes on your own give you time to think about the plan we put together for you?"

"Oh, I've seen all I need to." And then he did something incredibly stupid. He reached across the table and covered my hand with his, using his thumb to stroke my knuckles. "I think we're going to work together very well."

Oh, goody. Harassment.

The worst part was, I couldn't stab him with my fork the way reflex demanded I do. Not if I wanted to continue working. It didn't take much to spread ugly gossip. I, of all people, knew that. And there weren't many more dangerous egos than the ones belonging to actors.

Withdrawing my hand, I maintained a weak smile to keep the mood light. "Let's be careful," I warned. "That's the sort of thing that had your agent reaching out to me in the first place, remember?"

His laughter was warm and affable as he offered a helpless shrug. "Can't blame a guy for trying."

Were they all the same? I was starting to think so. It seemed like I was too young to feel so cynical, but the only other option was naïveté, which I couldn't afford.

We made plans to chat the following week, closer to the opening of his latest film, which happened to coincide with starting rehearsals for his upcoming play. I would be working overtime trying to monitor the goings-on with his leading lady since he was notorious for having flings with his costars. Again, the reason he needed me. There were some pretty pissed-off boyfriends and husbands back in California, and his agent didn't want the same mess erupting in New York.

Thanks to the gnawing in my stomach, it was a shame I couldn't focus on the thrill of signing a new client. Fucking Noah. It was like he got off on trying to make me feel small, the way he did back in the day—looking down at me, laughing at me, and treating me like a child. It was the same now, only I wasn't a little girl. He didn't know half of what he thought he did.

The thought of it had my blood pressure at an all-time high by the time I reached the spin studio for the class scheduled after my lunch meeting. I had stuck to salad to keep from feeling too full while working out. At the time, I figured that would be my biggest problem this afternoon.

Stupid me, forgetting how Noah tended to pop up to ruin even a good day. It was sort of his thing.

Aria wasn't around when I finished changing in the locker room. At first, I was concerned, but then I remembered the text she'd sent earlier in the morning about not being able to make it to class today.

I was that pissed off over Noah accusing me of flirting with a client. After he'd practically eye fucked Gretchen all through the interview earlier in the week. He had the nerve to act like he had no idea what I was talking about when I accused him of the same thing.

If anything, I was glad he'd decided to act like such a prick. It reminded me of everything wrong with him, which was something I needed to remember after feeling so jealous of Gretchen. He wasn't worth my jealousy. He was barely worth the oxygen he used to survive. I couldn't give him that power over me.

At the same time, I couldn't get the image of his face out of my mind as I battered my body, peddling until sweat rolled down the back of my neck and dripped from my chin. That bastard. The audacity to treat me like I was... well, no better than him.

I didn't feel any less bitter by the time we cooled down. No amount of exercise could get Noah off my mind or keep me from resenting him the way I did. To judge me, to make a fool out of me—again.

And dammit, I kept letting him do it. Why?

I had originally planned on going back to the office after my meeting, but considering I kept swinging back and forth between wanting to kill someone and wanting to cry out of sheer frustration, it seemed a better idea to go home and take care of whatever I could from there. Yes, I was letting Noah Goldsmith get to me. I hated it but felt powerless against it. And not powerless in that good way, like I felt at the club.

The club.

I couldn't get it out of my head. The memories would bubble to the surface when I least expected them, like now, on my way home with a gym bag over my shoulder and a true crime podcast playing in my AirPods. Not even the most gruesome mass murder was enough to ease the churning sensation in my gut.

Only one thing could. Was that true? Maybe, or perhaps I was telling myself that as an excuse to revisit the most incredible sexual experience of my life. Who was I kidding? He wouldn't be there, my mystery man. Unless there was another big party, I doubted there was any chance of running into him again.

The idea made my feet feel heavy as I dragged them through my apartment to the bedroom, chiding myself for being childish and taking unnecessary risks.

That didn't stop me from eyeing the bubblegum pink wig on my dresser and wondering if I should break her out again. I would just go to see if he was there. That was all.

Maybe I would have a drink.

Maybe I was coming up with excuses to return.

"Very well, Miss Black. You're all set." The intimidatingly beautiful girl behind the reception desk finished processing my payment before collecting my purse and phone to lock away under the counter. "Have a lovely evening."

I couldn't believe it. I had paid a membership fee to revisit Club Caramel. Until now, I could tell myself it was only a casual, passing interest sort of thing. Once money changed hands, it was a different story.

It wasn't like I couldn't afford it, even if I never came back. Nobody behind the desk batted an eye at the fact I was wearing a mask as I had before. In fact, my anxiety lessened a little when I entered the main room and found a few guests also in disguise. It made sense. Party or no party, there was still a little bit of a stigma around this kind of business. Even though we were all there together and, therefore, just as open to scandal if we outed each other, we felt like we had to hide.

My hunch was right. It was a lot quieter this time, though a few dozen people were getting a start on the evening. Since it was still early, there wasn't a lot of action going on. I knew once the liquor started flowing and inhibitions dropped away, it would be a different story.

I ordered a dirty martini at the bar, self-consciously adjusting the corset I wore over a pair of tight leather pants. Not a true corset, but it gave the right effect, pushing my boobs up until they were practically a shelf I could carry a drink on. The pants fit like a second skin, tucked into knee-high boots. It was very tame compared to the wild outfits and costumes worn by other members. Some people chose to change in the club's locker rooms to avoid being seen in their club wear outside the premises.

Discretion was key.

I could appreciate that, especially since my nerves were jangling, even with vodka entering my system. What if he didn't show up? That was possible, even probable. Still, there had to be part of me holding onto a shred of hope, or else I wouldn't be here.

I sipped the martini, observing a demonstration of various punishment techniques going on at the far end of the dance floor. That was one thing I wouldn't have expected—the amount of technique behind the sort of activities I'd always figured came naturally.

How many ways could a person be spanked? As it turned out, there was plenty I didn't know. "You want to be careful not to strike up here," the latex-clad instructor explained, hands against the lower back of his partner. "You don't want to damage the kidneys." I never would've thought of that. There was a lot more to this than I had imagined, and it had me paying closer attention to the demonstration as it went on.

Until...

The hair on the back of my neck lifted, and goose bumps raced across my skin. I didn't have to look to know I was being watched and didn't need proof of who was watching me. I felt it just as my body came alive—skin tingling, going warm all over, my heart fluttering before I ever turned my head to find a familiar stranger eyeing me up from the other end of the bar.

Like me, he wore a mask, making me wonder who he was in real life that he felt the need to disguise himself. His dark hair was slicked back away from his forehead, and his finely sculpted mouth curved into a knowing grin.

The rest of the room melted away, going hazy and vague, all my attention focused on him. I wanted to know him— who he was, why he was here, and why we were drawn to each other. I could barely breathe when his lips parted to emit what looked like a sigh. It was exquisite agony, hanging in midair, waiting to see what would happen next.

Instinctively knowing he was calling the shots.

He turned his head, looking toward the open door leading to the room we had visited before. A silent request, or was it a challenge? Either way, I wouldn't refuse.

Still, I didn't want to look too eager. I was shaking with anticipation, which meant it was smart to take my time, sliding from my barstool and walking down the length of the bar to where he waited. Like before, he was dressed in black, without anything that might set him apart from virtually any other man in the city.

I couldn't have picked him out of a line-up if he was dressed in street clothes, maskless. I liked it that way. The added layer of mystery deepened my interest, my pulse racing in anticipation by the time he raised a hand and touched a finger to his lips. *No talking.* I nodded, eager to get started, relieved when he pushed away from the bar and began leading the way to whatever the night had in store.

12

NOAH

The anticipation was almost too much.

The promise of what was to come.

Adrenaline flooded my system before we reached the private chamber, set up the way it was during our first encounter. I barely took the time to notice our surroundings when it was much more interesting looking at her, admiring the way those tight pants showed off her ass and her lacy corset top displayed her tits like a prize.

Saliva flooded my mouth in time with the surge of blood to my cock, standing it on end. The energy was electric and the atmosphere tense. With my back to the door and the mystery woman standing in the center of the room, I held up a finger and swirled it in a circle.

Turn around.

She did as I commanded, turned in a slow circle, then faced me again with her hands at her sides. She couldn't hide from me. Her teeth sank into her bottom lip while uncertainty flashed in her blue eyes, made even bluer thanks to the black lace that framed them.

While she watched, I reached down to what already

strained against my zipper, demanding to be freed. Her gaze lowered, and she watched me stroke myself through my pants, biting her lip harder than before.

Was she hungry for my cock?

She would have to wait. Her eyes widened as I approached, but she stayed still, holding her ground, almost like she was daring herself to stand firm under the force of what was undeniable.

I continued rubbing my bulge, reaching for her with my other hand. The first contact of my fingertips made her shiver as they gently grazed her jaw before trailing down her slim neck and across her collarbone. She swayed slightly, leaned toward me, and gave herself to me.

All at once, I cupped one of her tits, my touch now rough and possessive. Her surprised gasp ended with a sigh. She was made for me, that much was obvious. All she needed was someone who knew how to handle her.

Forgetting my painfully erect dick, I reached out and pulled her against me, sinking my fingers into her ass cheek until the leather of her pants squeaked. Her wide eyes met mine, full of questions and desire, but she offered no resistance as I backed her against a long bench jutting diagonally from one corner of the room.

Taking her by the hips, I spun her around, pressing a hand against the center of her back to position her across the bench, ass in the air. She sucked in another surprised gasp when I yanked her pants down to her knees. Her legs were bare, her skin covered in goose bumps. She tensed at the touch of my hands against the back of her thighs, and for a moment, it was enough to tease both of us, to leave her hanging and full of questions.

There was so much we could do.

So much I wanted to do to her.

The presence of a table full of dildos, vibrators, and other toys made my imagination race. I backed away, admiring her creamy ass cheeks and the red lace thong that disappeared between them. Perfect, succulent, and all mine.

For tonight, anyway.

It was gratifying that she stayed in place, waiting for me while I perused the toys. Aside from a glance over her shoulder, she didn't move, something I would have to reward her for.

But first, I caressed her ass cheeks with the end of a riding crop. There was something hypnotic about the sight of the black leather against her white skin. It wouldn't be so white for long.

She tensed at the first tap against her cheek. I gave her time to adjust, striking the other cheek, moving back and forth, increasing the force a little at a time, warming her up and turning her flesh pink. It would be sensitive now. Sure enough, when I offered the softest caress, she released a moan. Now that the blood rushed to the surface, she would feel everything so much more intensely.

"Shh..." I reminded her, adding a sharper strike to drive the point home. She gasped but took it, and I tested her by using the same force again and again, seeing how far I could take it before she broke and cried out. It was clear she wanted to, but she went no further than a strained whimper while I turned her ass tomato red. It seemed strange that I would be proud of her, but I was, smiling by the time welts began to rise over the formerly smooth surface.

The real fun started when I stroked her ass with a featherlight touch. Her back arched like she'd been shocked, and her hips rolled in circles. The sensation would be unbearable by now, and her shuddering breaths and shaking body betrayed the almost painful pleasure I subjected her to.

It wasn't enough.

She needed more.

She deserved more for submitting so beautifully to me, bending to my will without saying a word.

She flinched when the buzzing started, then sighed as I ran a small vibrator over her quivering ass. I was careful to keep it away from her crack even as she arched her back to present herself, silently begging me to offer relief. Instead, I teased her thighs and cheeks until she was shaking from the effort of holding herself back. By the time I ran the tip of the vibrator between her ass cheeks, her juices glistened even in the dim lighting.

She'd soaked through her thong.

Slowly, I lowered the lacy scrap, leaving it around her knees along with her pants before tracing her plump, moistened lips with the vibrator. Her breathing was quick, ragged, her ass moving up and down as she tried to find relief from the tension by forcing me to touch the vibrator to her clit.

Fuck, I could smell her arousal, could feel the heat of her pussy by the time I trained the toy on her swollen bundle of nerves.

I was her god, and right then, I held her life in my hands. That was how she would feel as I toyed with her, pulling back whenever she was too close to coming. Her high-pitched whimpers drove me deeper into pleasuring her.

Did she think that would earn her sympathy? My soft chuckles made her whine, a sound that was cut off when I pulled the vibrator away entirely. She settled down, stilling immediately. She was getting the message.

Rewarding her obedience, I pressed the vibrator tight against her clit, turning up the intensity until the sound nearly drowned out her harsh breathing. That was the only sound she made until the tension broke. She came silently, shaking from the effort before going limp over the bench.

We weren't finished.

Not even close.

Sliding the vibrator through her slit, I spread her juices from clit to asshole before plunging the vibrator inside her still-quivering cunt. She gasped before going still, sucking in one ragged breath after another. I didn't know if she was building to another orgasm or if she hadn't yet finished the first. She was lost in sensation, that much was for sure.

I ran a thumb around her puckered asshole, adding to that. I wouldn't take it, but I enjoyed letting her think other-wise, applying pressure with the pad of my thumb while working the vibrator in and out of her dripping sheath. Fuck, she was hot, pushing back against me, grunting softly. A work of art, and all for me.

I couldn't take it anymore. My dick was so hard it hurt, coated in precum by the time I pulled it from my boxers. The rhythm of my strokes soon matched that of the vibrator. In and out, my breathing growing faster the closer she came to coming again.

For me.

All for me.

By the time she was ready to explode, I buried the vibrator deep and left it there, hurrying my way through pulling a condom from my back pocket and unrolling it over my length. In one quick move, I pulled the vibrator free and replaced it with my cock.

Her grunt of satisfaction drove me onward, leaving me to take her by the hips and holding them in place.

How could I forget how tight she was?

Hot, wet, wrapped around my cock like she was built for me. Like I was where I belonged.

Inside her.

Closing my eyes, I adjusted to the thrilling sensation until the impulse to come passed. She was that good.

I wasn't gentle and didn't take my time. I fucked her, plain and simple, rutting like an animal the way I wanted it. I forgot everything else, letting my primal needs take over releasing my frustrations, uncertainties, and everything weighing on my mind. I gave it to her and poured it into her with every thrust and wet slap of skin on skin.

And she took it. She took it so fucking willingly.

By the time she clenched around me, I was dangerously close, her greedy pussy trying to milk me dry. Rather than let go, I withdrew, unrolling the condom as I rounded the bench.

"Open," I whispered, aiming for her mouth. She raised her head and obeyed, her mouth hanging open, her tongue extended. Our eyes met in the split second before the rush overtook me, and I recognized the satisfaction I saw there before my cum coated her waiting tongue. She swallowed my load, and I closed my eyes, satisfied.

Everything was as it should be by the time I opened them, my dick now softening, my muscles trembling. The slate had been wiped clean. I was a new man.

A new man in the presence of a woman who now stood to pull up her pants, avoiding my gaze while she did. The moment was over, the way it needed to be, and I pulled myself together once I'd caught my breath. Disappointment threatened to overwhelm me when she turned away, prepared to make a quick exit the way I had before, but I kept a lid on it.

What difference did it make whether I wanted to spend the rest of the night ravishing her? Tasting her pussy, sucking her tits until she moaned my name? We couldn't do that. She couldn't know my name any more than I could know hers.

Yet I couldn't give her up.

It was childish to think we could keep going like this, visiting the club on the off chance we would find each other. I had never felt this completely relaxed and renewed after a good, hard fuck. She was the missing ingredient. Somehow, she instinctively understood what I needed just as I knew what would make her come until her legs shook.

Was I telling myself what I needed to believe? I didn't take time to examine the question, heading out to the main floor with one goal in mind—finding her, catching up to her, and learning who she was. It was risky, but what was life without a little risk?

She was fast. I scanned the room, searching for that bubblegum pink hair. By the time I found her bobbing head, she was already on her way out, heading for the lobby in a hurry to get out of there now that she'd been satisfied.

I couldn't make it look like I was stalking her, even if that was my intention. The bouncers positioned throughout the club would notice and stop me. I was caught between needing to catch her and needing to avoid being kicked out for good.

I would never find her that way.

Somehow, I got lucky. A handful of people were on their way out, waiting for their belongings at the front counter. She joined them, and I watched from the doorway as one of the girls behind the counter unlocked the drawer containing guests' personal items.

All it took was one look at her phone for my insides to go cold and my mind to go blank for a moment before reality slammed into me. The force of my realization made me fall back a step, reeling, unable to process what was in front of my face.

I knew that phone or rather the case it was in. I had seen it enough times, the shining gold obvious even in the discreet near-dark of the front lobby.

Fuck, she even smelled the same as she had earlier, in front of the restaurant—vanilla and what I now realized was lavender. Even while she wore that wig, I could smell it on her when we were close but didn't make the connection until now. How could I have missed what now seemed so obvious?

I was no longer looking at a stranger. I was looking at Sienna Black.

I had fucked Sienna Black.

Twice.

And I knew before I took another breath that I needed to do it again.

13

SIENNA

"Of course, journalists can't reveal their sources."

The silence following that comment made me realize Lucy was waiting for my response. I had been staring out the window, remembering my most recent visit to Club Caramel and wondering if I should go back while my senior staff member got me up to speed on the finer points of Noah's account.

Looking her way, I felt guilty for not giving her my full attention. "We need to keep digging," I insisted. "Unless we learn who made these allegations, we can't guarantee they won't make more."

Her mouth screwed up in an expression of uneasiness. "On the other hand, everything's going according to plan on our end. They're going to see that what they did had a little lasting impact. What's in it for them, doubling down? They'll look ridiculous if they keep this up."

Normally, I might have agreed with her point. This client was anything but normal. "What's more important to them? Not looking ridiculous or making sure the world hates Noah Goldsmith?"

"We'll keep digging," she promised, making a note. "Otherwise, his entire social media presence has been cleaned up, and we have some nice throwback posts scheduled. The family photos he sent over, that kind of thing. Reminding the world he's just a normal guy."

A normal guy with a massive trust fund and a nearly billion-dollar company. So relatable. But that was the nature of the business. "Excellent. I'm sure he'll be happy to hear about that when he comes in." The mere thought made me quake inside.

She perked up like a freshly watered plant. "I would be more than happy to speak with him if you want."

Why was there a sudden, stabbing sensation in my chest? Considering Lucy's team had taken over most of the work pertaining to Noah, it made sense for her to meet with him rather than taking time from my busy schedule.

Memories of that interview in his penthouse and the flirting that took place made up my mind. "No, that's fine. We need to catch up, anyway." It hadn't quite been a week since we'd faced off on Park Avenue with Jacob waiting for me inside the restaurant, and since then, Noah had kept his distance. I should've been glad and grateful, but then so little about our relationship went the way it should have. Rather than thank my lucky stars he was busy bothering somebody else, I was almost irked by his silence. I couldn't win when it came to him.

Rather than let him flirt shamelessly with Lucy, I would face him like the adult I was. I had good news for him, positive developments to share. With any luck, it would be a good, short meeting, and we would leave feeling satisfied.

Amazing, the things I told myself.

It was clear when Noah entered the room a few minutes after Lucy left that this would not go how I hoped. It wasn't that he came in guns blazing, throwing his attitude around, but quite the opposite. He was quiet, reserved, almost surprisingly polite as he greeted me. "I thought I would check out my social media accounts to get an idea of what your team has been doing," he explained after taking a seat, arranging himself in the chair across from me. Rather than his typical suit, he wore a charcoal turtleneck snug enough to outline his muscular arms and shoulders.

Good Lord.

We were barely a minute into the meeting, and I needed a cold shower.

I swallowed hard. "I'm glad you're happy. I understand we're posting your family photos soon. It was nice of you to send them over and to grant the team access to your accounts."

Lifting a thick shoulder, he said, "It's the least I could do."

What the hell was happening? He wouldn't stop staring at me while wearing something halfway between a knowing smirk and a full grin—he look of a man who was in on a joke. The only problem was it was one I was unaware of.

He looked away for a second, and I looked down at myself, expecting to find a piece of food on my boobs or something like that. I even ran a quick hand under my nose, then touched the corners of my mouth in case something lingered there from breakfast.

"I wanted to talk to you about the sports clinic." Because we were here for business, not for me to question every choice I made this morning, thanks to Noah's strange attitude.

I knew better than to expect an apology for his bullshit tantrum last week, but this about-face made my skin crawl in an eerie way. Maybe somebody had talked sense to him, convinced him to be an adult. It occurred to me I could ask him straight-out, but I didn't want to give him the impression I was too hung up on every little thing he said and did. It would be better to let it go and move forward.

I slid a folder across the desk. "Most of the information is in there. I made arrangements with a Boys and Girls Club in the Bronx. A group of kids ranging from ages ten to twelve will be participating. It's a one-day event. We'll have a handful of baseball, football, and basketball players spending time with the kids. The first half of the day will be dedicated to throwing the balls around, that sort of thing. After lunch, the guys will talk about sportsmanship, dedication, mindset, and that sort of thing. At the end of the day, you'll present a check to the Boys and Girls Club representative and get photos with the kids."

I was talking to a wall. He nodded slowly, and I watched his eyes move over the pages as he flipped through the information packet, but he may as well have been a robot, completely without reaction. Something about it left me jittery. "We are also looking into the source of that article if you're still interested in that," I ventured in a louder voice. Something had to get a reaction out of him, right?

He snickered, at least. "I'm telling you, look no further than Drake Thomas. It had to be him." But even that didn't carry any emotion. Noah had barely kept himself from throwing blows with Drake at the foundation gala, but now he didn't seem to care.

It wasn't long before I couldn't take it anymore. "Is everything all right with you?" I blurted out. "Or is there a problem with the family? With Rose, maybe?"

This time, he reacted, his brows drawing together and his head snapping back in surprise. "Where did that come from? Everyone's fine, as far as I know. What, do you know something I don't?"

"Generally, yes." And I didn't know what was worse. The fact that I blurted it out before I knew what I was doing or his reaction. The Noah I thought I knew would have growled at me or muttered some snarky response. This Noah, the bizarro version who could be an alien replacement for all I knew, merely chuckled.

"I've turned over a new leaf." Closing the folder, he left it on the desk, settling back and wearing an easygoing smirk. "I guess I have you to thank for that."

This was all wrong.

The ugliest flashback hit me at the worst possible time. I was fifteen again, standing at my family's apartment door while he smirked down at me. He was in on the joke, and I was about to be caught in the crossfire. Was that what was going on now? Could I afford to take a chance and assume good intentions?

I bristled, rolling my shoulders back. "You're going to have to explain yourself because I'm not liking how this is going."

Then I stood, crossing the room to grab something cold from the mini refrigerator in the corner. I was entirely too warm, too unsettled. And it gave me the opportunity to collect myself while he wasn't staring into my face.

"Exactly what am I doing wrong?" he asked. "Trying to patch things up so we can have a good working relationship, and you're still treating me like a fuckup." Even that came off wrong since he sounded like he was making a joke. There was no growling, grunting, or grinding of teeth.

"Out with it already." I twisted the cap on a bottle of green juice, glaring at him over my shoulder before taking a swig of the drink. I barely tasted it. It may as well have been sawdust. After swallowing, I announced, "You're fucking with me, and I don't like it. I also don't have time for it."

My heart lodged itself in my throat when he stood, unfolding his impressive body. He moved slowly toward me, his hands in his pockets and his eyes flicking over my face before skimming over my form-fitting dress. "Why does everything have to be a fight with you?" His voice was softer, deeper, and it did dangerous things to my pussy while also kicking my instincts into high gear. "I'm trying to be decent to make up for the shit I already put you through. Is that a crime?"

No, but it was all wrong. Did he forget we hadn't just met? "You know, an apology would work just as well."

Scoffing, he muttered, "I don't do apologies."

"Wow. I'm shocked."

"Besides. What are words?" He looked me over again, pulling his hands from his pockets and making me wonder what he planned on doing with them while he stepped up close enough to give me a whiff of his toe-curling cologne. "I'm much more into action. And I think you are too."

Sexy cologne or not, this was entirely too unnerving. "I don't know what you think you're doing, but—"

A wicked smile flashed across his face before he touched a finger to his lips. "Shh."

No.

It wasn't possible.

All the air left my lungs in a rush before nausea twisted my stomach. So this was how it felt when the entire world came crashing down like cold sweat prickling on the back of my neck while I fought with all my might to deny what was in front of me.

Once again, I was back where I started—at a loss, fumbling around in my head, panicking while he stood in front of me, practically on the verge of laughter. At least, that was how it looked while I fought to keep down what I had just drank.

It was impossible.

It couldn't be true.

Yet when I looked at him, when I truly saw him, it was painfully obvious. His height, his physique, his mouth and eyes. All of it. It was him. It had been him all along, and he knew it.

"Get out." My voice was shaking, but I didn't care. Fuck, he had already seen me in the most intimate, almost embarrassing moments. What difference did it make now if I showed a little emotion? "Get out of my office and never come back."

His smile slipped, and he had the nerve to look surprised. "Wait. That's not how this is supposed to be."

"I don't give a damn what you think this is supposed to be," I spat. I could barely hear my voice over the roaring in my head.

How could he? How could he know and make a joke about it? How long had he known? The entire time? Why wouldn't he say anything?

I didn't have it in me to demand answers and wasn't sure I could bear hearing them anyway. Not when I was on the verge of a screaming, sobbing fit. How could he do this? How could he take advantage of me that way? I could've died from shame then and there while he gaped at me in surprise.

"Do I need to call security?" I whispered, shaking, on the verge of tears.

"This isn't right," he insisted. "It wasn't supposed to—"

"I said go. *Now,* Noah," I insisted, thrusting a shaking

arm toward the door. "Or I will have you escorted out. Your choice."

A range of conflicting emotions washed over him, playing across his chiseled features before those features hardened into an unreadable mask. "Right. Whatever you say." He had the nerve to scoff as he turned away and crossed the room, shaking his head the whole way.

I barely managed to hold myself together until he was gone. Once the door closed, I staggered to my desk, leaning against it with one hand on my chest. Every breath took effort while my heart raced out of control, and the room spun around me.

It was *him.*

It was him all along.

I had been fantasizing about him, touching myself to the memory of him, wondering if I would ever find anyone to make me come the way he did or if I should've asked who he was so we could reconnect.

And even as I broke down and let the tears fall, I didn't know why I was crying. Was it that he had found a way to make a fool of me again or that I knew this meant our last encounter was the last encounter?

Because I would never leave myself vulnerable to him again as long as I lived.

14

NOAH

"Thanks for checking on me, *Dad*," I grumbled, tapping my fingers on the steering wheel and asking myself why I hadn't taken the private jet instead of driving.

Traffic was a nightmare on the way into East Hampton.

"Hey, don't blame me," Colton insisted, his voice filling the car's interior. "It was your sister who made me call to check on you. Everybody else is here already. She worried you were in an accident." He chuckled before adding, "I told her it was more likely you got distracted by some hot redhead."

I couldn't bring myself to laugh at my best friend's joke. "Don't send out the search parties for me. I'm stuck in traffic, is all. You said everyone's already there?"

"The whole group. We're planning a bonfire out on the beach tonight. Lucian and Evan went out to make sure we were stocked with everybody's favorite booze. The girls are excited about making us a big dinner."

All of the girls? If I asked, he would know something was off. Normally, having the group at my parents' estate for the weekend would be a no-brainer. I would be there in a heartbeat, especially now that Colton spent so much time with my sister. Rose probably felt the same way about a weekend with her girls, hence the reason for her bullying all of us into coming out.

What a shame Sienna was one of the girls.

"Get here in one piece!" Rose shouted from somewhere nearby.

"Will do," I assured her before ending the call.

If Sienna were a no-show, I would've heard about it by now. There was no way around it—we'd have to see each other.

I would've looked forward to it if it wasn't for the way she broke down in her office.

My fingers tapped faster than before as the car inched down the 495. This gave me time to think, even if sitting in an endless line of vehicles was about as much fun as having my teeth pulled.

This would be the first time I saw or spoke to her since the disaster three days ago.

I shouldn't have done it. How was I supposed to know she would take it the way she did? There I was, thinking we would have something in common, a shared secret, that we might even...

I shook my head at the ridiculousness, growling when the thought entered my mind again. *We could even get together again without the disguises this time.*

She could've given me the chance to explain myself. That, I couldn't forgive. I'd wanted to tell her how surprised I was when I realized who I had just fucked, that she didn't have to worry, and it would be our secret. She could trust me. Let's face it, I had as much to lose as she did if word of my extracurricular activities got out.

Sienna wouldn't give me the chance because she'd decided I wasn't worth it a long time ago. I could almost consider thanking her for setting me straight. I'd allowed my dick to think for me yet again, and it left me with the stupid idea that we could take our physical relationship outside the club.

I was supposed to know better than that and be beyond sleeping with the same woman more than once. After a few failed attempts at something close to relationships in college, I'd made the same decision my friends had—there was nothing to be gained from being tied down.

Colton had since changed his mind, but that didn't make a difference. We couldn't all find a special someone.

By the time I turned my Bentley onto the familiar wide driveway leading up to the mansion, it was well past seven o'clock, and night had fallen. A crisp night, clear skies, good for a bonfire. What a shame I wouldn't be able to enjoy it.

When all was said and done, no matter how wrong it was and how I questioned what the fuck had happened to my brain, there was no avoiding the truth. I couldn't forget what happened between us.

Hell, I didn't want to.

I wasn't going to give up the way Sienna expected. Not when it was so fucking good. Not only for me, either. She couldn't deny what I did to her body. She couldn't pretend it was easy to walk away from that.

There was one thing I felt secure in as I pulled a bag from the back seat and jogged up the front stairs—I didn't have to worry about her exposing us to anyone. Not a chance. As far as everyone else was concerned, nothing had changed. I was confident enough in that to stroll into the house like nothing was wrong and call out, "Somebody pour me a fucking drink!"

The shouts coming from the kitchen drew me in that direction. I soon picked up the aroma of onions and garlic, which grew stronger the closer I drew.

"There you are!" Evan called out, sitting with his feet up on the long marble-topped table on the far side of the room. "Thank fuck, I'm starving."

"Well, then, that was worth sitting in traffic for," I muttered back, then flipped him off before accepting a hug from my sister, Rose.

"The usual, I assume?" Colton placed a glass of scotch in front of me on the island countertop before wrapping his arms around Rose's waist. Would I threaten to kick his ass ever again, the way I did when I first found out about them? No, especially not when they were so into each other. Still, the sight of them cuddling always jarred me a little at first, even after three months.

"You should've taken the jet with us," Valentina reminded me. Either she didn't feel like cooking or didn't know how. I would've bet on the latter since she sat on the counter with a glass of red wine, picking at Rose's chopped vegetables for a big salad rather than contributing.

"I'll know better next time." I wanted the freedom to leave when I felt like it. I didn't expect things to go south, but I wanted to be prepared.

As it was, Sienna hadn't acknowledged me. Something about stirring sautéed vegetables was too fascinating, requiring her full attention. She only moved when Aria nudged her aside, sliding a tray of rolls into the oven.

If anything, I appreciated being ignored. It wasn't far beyond the way things usually went between us anyway. She'd already hated me before we ever set eyes on each other at the club.

Lucian came in from the back patio with a platter of

grilled chicken and salmon. It was easier and safer to gravitate toward the guys, bullshitting while the girls put the finishing touches on the meal. I stood with my back to them, which helped me resist the temptation to admire the way Sienna's leggings fit her like a second skin and made her ass look more delectable than ever.

Sadly, there was no getting her off my mind.

"So, any slander thrown your way lately?" Lucian asked.

Busting balls was what we did best, so I let it go with nothing more than an eye roll. "Not recently. Things are going well."

"Because Sienna kicks ass at what she does!" Aria chirped from across the room. Why she couldn't be more reserved like her twin sister, Valentina, was beyond me.

I wanted to ask who the fuck was talking to her but bit my tongue. The girls cheered behind me, and I did my best to look like a normal person with a lot to be grateful for, which I was—all things considered. Aside from our personal issues, things were turning out better than I had imagined and on a faster timeline.

It was a relief when Evan changed the subject to what we would do in the morning, a conversation that carried us into the meal.

Did anyone notice how far Sienna went out of her way to keep from talking to me, looking at me, or acknowledging my presence across the table? It had to be my knowledge of the situation that made her behavior more obvious. Everyone else seemed to overlook it, even Rose, who knew her best.

She couldn't keep this up forever. That was what I told myself as I half-heartedly helped clean up, then went outside with the guys to light the bonfire. Lucian and Evan carried a cooler while the girls trailed behind us with blankets once the fire was blazing. Their laughter floated from behind us as they descended the stairs leading down to the sand. So long as I wasn't in Sienna's face, she could be happy, and for some reason, I wanted that for her.

I stared out over the moonlight-painted water, my thoughts churning.

"Oh shit!"

I turned away from the water and found Sienna in the sand at the base of the stairs, gripping her ankle. "I only rolled it," she told the girls as they gathered around. Colton jogged over too." You all right, sis?"

She waved him off. "I'm fine. For real."

Why did she look my way? "But... I might go up, anyway. I would rather do it now than later if it gets swollen. I'll come back down in a while if it feels better."

So long as I don't have to be around Noah. I could see straight through her.

"There's plenty of ice in the cooler to make you a pack," Colton pointed out, but she wasn't hearing it as she got on her feet, favoring the left ankle.

"I'll help you up to the house," I offered, approaching with an arm outstretched. "I left my flask up there, anyway. I'm glad I thought to bring it so I wouldn't have to drink the cheap shit Evan bought," I added, shouting over my shoulder and cueing up laughter.

Sienna didn't laugh. "No, that's fine." She tried to back away, but it was no use. She would look ridiculous if she insisted on hobbling up the steps on her own. I draped her arm over my shoulders and started up the stairs with my arm around her waist.

She wouldn't say a word as I helped her hop from one step to the next. How could she when she was busy grunting and huffing angrily? "Were you planning on ignoring me all weekend?" I asked once we had put some distance between us and the group.

"Shut up. I'm not in the mood." Her voice was icy, empty. Now I understood there was something more intense than being hated. It was flat indifference.

"Somebody's going to figure out you've got a problem with me. What are you going to say?"

"Nobody will notice. I thought I asked you to shut up." We reached the patio spanning half of the house's east side, where she tried to push me away. "I'm fine now. I'll go up to my room."

"Let me help you up there," I offered, caught between fucking with her and wanting very much to have the excuse to get her in the bedroom.

She flushed in the light flowing out from the kitchen. "That's unnecessary."

Fuck this. I wasn't going to beg, and I wouldn't help her when she insisted on being so fucking stubborn.

"Fine. Crawl up the stairs for all I care." I continued without her, marching across the flagstone patio and flinging open one of the French doors leading into the kitchen. My flask was in my bag, which I left in the entry hall to carry up later.

She took considerably more time to reach the curved staircase leading to the second floor, but I pretended not to notice as I went through my things. By the time I found the flask of Macallan, she had managed to hobble up five stairs out of many more.

I knew what I should do, no matter how tempting it was to let her screw herself over since that's what she was determined to do. "I don't need your help." She sounded weaker than before, and she didn't believe herself no matter what she said.

"Which room did you take?" I asked with an arm around her waist and began helping her hop from one step to the next without paying attention to her protests. Eventually, I lost patience, ignoring her ineffectual arguing in favor of lifting her off her feet and carrying her the rest of the way.

"This is stupid!" she groaned out.

"It was either that or spend the rest of the night helping you get upstairs, and I have better things to do."

She pointed down the hall to one of the guest rooms, and I headed there, not letting her go until we were inside the spacious room across the hall from the room I'd always used. Rose had seen to it the space was aired out, with fresh linens on the bed and fragrant flowers on the nightstand.

"Okay. Put me down." Her insistence irritated me worse than ever. What the hell was her problem? I had heard of people cutting off their noses to spite their faces, but she was taking it to the next level.

Still, electricity was in the air when I set her on the bed. "Let me take a look at this," I offered, one hand on her calf, lifting her leg so I could observe her swelling ankle. "There's probably bandages or something around here. You might've sprained it, but you can still move it. I doubt it's broken."

"Thank you, *Doctor*." She pulled herself free of my grip and propped on her elbows, glaring up at me. If she only knew how irresistible she was when her eyes flashed and her cheeks flushed, not to mention she was practically sprawled out across the bed.

My dick stirred at the sight of her. "Want me to rub it for you?"

"I want you to leave me alone." It didn't sound that way. Her words were hollow, weak, almost whispered. "Please. Be decent and leave me alone."

"Decency has never been my strong suit."

"Shit. I already knew that before you threw the club in my face." When all I could do was gape at her, she rolled her eyes. "In my office. Don't pretend that's not what you were trying to do."

"I'm not pretending." I stepped up close to the bed until my knees brushed the duvet, and she had no choice but to spread her legs to make room for me. Oh, she was so tempting. "Now I get it. You thought I was making fun? That's what you think of me?"

"Could we not turn this into—"

I shook my head, reaching down to take hold of her knees and hold them apart while I leaned down, my eyes locked on her. Her baby blues widened, her head pulling back until it practically touched the bed, brown locks fanning out around her. "Let me make one thing clear. I was not interested in making a fool out of you, and I'm not interested in it now. Next time you're confused about something I say or do, talk to me about it instead of throwing me out before I can explain. Understood?"

Eyes narrowing, she asked, "What do you think you're doing? Don't talk to me that way."

In a flash, I reached down and slid a hand under her head, pulling it toward me until our mouths nearly brushed. Her short, quick breaths hit my face while mine did the same to hers. "I asked if you understand. Yes or no?"

She gulped but gave me a slight nod. "Yes."

"Good girl." Hunger roared inside me. Fuck, I was touching her again, smelling her skin, feeling her warmth. So far, I had exercised self-control, refusing the intimacy of a kiss. Yet when her tantalizing lips parted, I was nearly knocked on my ass by the sudden, undeniable urge to taste them.

"Not that easy," she informed me in a shaky whisper.

"You can't say a few words and think it will change anything."

"Then again, we've never needed words, have we?" My hand slid up her thigh, gliding over the soft leggings she wore, while the fingers of my other hand slid through her soft hair. "We did just fine without them before. Unless you faked it when you came all over my cock."

She sucked in a sharp breath, shuddering. "Don't talk about that."

"Is that going to erase the past? Pretending it didn't happen? Do you honestly think you could forget how good it was? You loved it. Don't lie to yourself, especially not to me." I groaned, pressing my fingers against her supple flesh. "You're getting wet right now, aren't you, Sienna? Admit it. You can't handle being this close to me any more than I can handle being close to you."

Her brows drew together, almost like she was in pain. "You don't need to be." Who did she think she was kidding? She was trembling again, the innocent fawn cowering in the face of what she couldn't resist.

"Then tell me to get away. But make me believe it," I added when she took a breath, prepared to do just that, and her arguments dissolved into nothing but a whimper. She couldn't lie to me or herself, and she knew it.

It was too much. I couldn't fight it another second, not when she was right there, helpless in the face of what we shared. What she couldn't forget. What I didn't want to forget.

The first touch of her lips was a rush, going straight to my head and making it spin while a flash of heat came close to melting my skin off. At the same time, it was so right, like slipping into an old pair of jeans. Something that fit so perfectly I couldn't do anything but stretch out on top of her before drinking in another kiss, then another.

She melted the way I knew she would, falling back against the bed, nails digging into my shoulders before running through my hair. My tongue stroked hers until she moaned into my mouth, a guttural sound that made my cock jump and twitch. With one leg wrapped around my hip, she pulled me close, her greedy body betraying her useless attempts at fighting the inevitable. We were never going to walk away like nothing happened. It wasn't possible. Not when the same electricity that had hummed between us sparked and crackled in the air as I rolled onto my side, and she went with me.

Her hips jerked, her pussy grinding against my covered cock, and I couldn't help but press my hand against her mound. Her desperate cry left me pressing harder, grinding the heel of my hand against her slit, which wasn't enough for either of us.

Our friends and family partied outside while I worked my fingers inside her leggings, finding the place where it was hot and wet, pushing aside the crotch of her panties to dip inside her sopping pussy.

"So wet for me," I rasped out after breaking the kiss to gulp in some air. She buried her face in my neck, nearly sobbing by the time I sank two fingers deep into her juicy cunt, working her clit with my thumb, playing her body like the exquisite instrument it was. Teasing her earlobe with my teeth, shuddering the way she did. "Are you going to come for me? Are you going to be my good girl and come over my fingers?"

She clung to me tighter, hips bucking, hot breath against my skin. "Yes!" she gasped out.

"You like the way I make your pussy feel?" Fuck, I would

come in my pants if this went on much longer, building her up with every stroke and word I whispered into her ear. "Tell me," I urged, stroking her G-spot while tracing circles over her bundle of nerves.

"Oh God!" she cried out, clawing at my back. "Yes... yes, I do! Oh, God, Noah, please!"

"Please what?" She was so close I could barely move my fingers once her muscles began to clench around them.

"Please, let me come!" she sobbed, fucking my fingers wildly. I liked her better this way, being able to hear her greedy desperation while I worked her body into a frenzy. There was nothing like the satisfaction of feeling her go stiff, hearing her breath catch in that last moment before she shuttered, trembled, and coated my palm with her juices. By the time I pulled my slick fingers free from her pussy, she whimpered and trembled against me.

"Good girl," I whispered in approval. "You come so well for me." She whimpered against my neck, wrapping her body around mine until I gritted my teeth against the desire to take her the way she so clearly wanted. Not here, not now, when anyone could disturb us. The thrill of fingering her was one thing, but I had to be smart enough to leave things where they were.

"Where are you going?" There was disappointment in the question when I sat up, leaving her alone.

"Back outside before anybody misses me. Take care of that ankle." If I didn't leave her then and there, the slim thread of self-control I clung to would snap. As it was, I barely made it across the hall to my room before my aching dick demanded release from my shorts.

I unzipped my khakis and shoved a hand inside my boxer briefs on the way to the attached bathroom, pulling my erect cock free. Precum coated the head, and I used it to fuck my fist, already close enough that the familiar tingle had begun at the base of my spine. I could see her in my mind's eye, still hear her moans, and smell her on my skin.

All at once, the rush came over me, and I went with it, spilling my seed in one spurt after another against a hand towel. By the time I finished, I was weak-kneed, leaning against the sink for support, my ragged breath the only sound in the otherwise empty room.

One thing was clear before I ever managed to catch my breath.

I would need to have her again and as soon as possible. She was the sort of habit a man couldn't break—not that I wanted to try.

15

SIENNA

If the past thirty-six hours had proven anything, it was how completely fucked up Noah had made me. I was so sure on the way out here that I could face ignoring him all weekend for the sake of keeping up appearances. It was safer that way. Besides, I had plenty of practice with it. I had honed my skills for a decade.

But then Friday night happened, and he had to go and touch me the way he did. He had to kiss me and melt all of my resistance. He had to wipe away all of my resentment and fear.

And then? He pretended none of it happened.

The push-and-pull power exchange that turned me on while we were at the club did the opposite in real life. Now, he was on top, and he let me know it by going out of his way to keep things cordial but distant in front of the rest of the group. He went out of his way to make sure we were never alone and barely made eye contact. Not because he was nervous or regretful. That wasn't Noah. I knew him better than that.

It was because, damn him, he had to know that little

orgasm had only woken up my appetite. There was no such thing as enough when it came to him and what he did to me.

He was going to make me work for more. I knew it the second I saw the raging boner jutting out when he got up from the bed. Only a man determined to torture me would walk away when he was that hard, not to mention I was so obviously willing.

Well, fuck that. Okay, so I knew he wasn't making fun back in my office. The time we'd had together wasn't a joke to him. Something good had come out of those wild moments stretched out on the guest bed.

But I wasn't about to beg, not even for cock or one as impressive as his. He was dead wrong if he thought playing games all weekend would work.

"Sienna, another mimosa?" Rose held up the bottle of champagne and the pitcher of orange juice, her eyebrows moving up and down. "You need to enjoy yourself a little this weekend."

"I'm good," I told her, shaking my head. I was still working on my first drink, and considering I planned on driving back to the city after brunch, it seemed a good idea to stick to one. "And it's not like I didn't have any fun at the spa or when we were shopping yesterday." It was safer to be with the girls only and easier to think without Noah's presence looming over everything. A tight bandage and ibuprofen every few hours allowed me to have a good time. Wine had also helped.

This morning marked another welcome break, having brunch with the girls at my family's house a few miles from the Goldsmith estate. I had jumped at Mom's offer to host us this morning. She was in town to meet with a new client at their home, and Dad never missed an excuse nowadays to get in some golf out here.

Sitting in the sunny kitchen, I felt comfortable. At home. Able to relax without Noah's presence reminding me of the huge secret we were keeping.

"You look tired, honey." Mom took my chin in one hand, looking down at me with her usual motherly concern. "Do you need another pillow under your ankle?"

It was already propped up on three pillows on a spare chair at the kitchen table. "I think I'm okay."

My father grumbled as he passed through the room, a pair of golf gloves sticking out from his khakis' back pocket. "I think you should have gone to get an X-ray," he reminded me for the fifth time since we had arrived.

Rose and the others giggled softly, exchanging knowing looks while I did what I could not roll my eyes at my parents' concern.

"I'm fine, Dad. It's just a sprain."

"Are you sure you'll be able to drive home? Let me have a car take you back. Your mother or I could drive the Mercedes to your building tomorrow."

"Thank you, but that's okay." I blew him a kiss after he shook his head at Mom before heading out for his tee time. Mom only sighed deeply before returning to the French toast she was frying for us. I loved them, but there were times when it seemed they forgot I was an adult.

Valentina snagged a ripe, ruby-red strawberry from the bowl of fruit on the table. "Do you need any extra help at that sports clinic you're holding next weekend?" she asked before taking a bite.

Aria nodded firmly, turning my way. "We'd be happy to keep those kids in line or whatever you need help with."

"I don't remember asking for help," I pointed out, barely

biting back a knowing smile at her transparency. "And I'm pretty sure those hot, rich, gorgeous pro athletes will be able to manage things themselves." Because obviously, that's where the concern came from.

Who didn't want to spend a day with a bunch of virile athletes? And everybody knew men grew exponentially hotter while interacting with kids. It was pretty much a law of nature.

"Okay, then maybe we'll come along to make sure you and Noah don't claw each other's eyes out." Valentina winked at my wide-eyed reaction. Unlike Aria, she stuck to her natural chestnut brown hair color, now twirling a strand around her finger. "I mean, there has to be a limit somewhere, right? I'm surprised you haven't killed him yet."

"We all know there's no love lost there," Rose pointed out, offering a sympathetic look as she flopped down next to me. "Even though it happened a long time ago, you don't forget that kind of thing."

Mom's phone rang, offering a distraction. "Hey, Liv," she called out after answering, heading through the back door to take Olivia's call on the porch.

It couldn't have come at a better time since my head was spinning, and a sense of unease took hold of me. I looked around the table at my twin cousins and best friend, waiting for an explanation as they exchanged uncomfortable glances.

"What thing are you talking about?" I asked Rose, narrowing my eyes. She couldn't fool me. The girl blushed at the drop of a hat, and the familiar shade of red was already creeping its way up her neck.

It was Aria who threw her hands in the air. "Enough's enough. We all know what happened with Pierce back in high school. It's so stupid, acting like we don't know about it ten years later. It was a long time ago."

"You knew about that? Oh, God," I groaned out, covering my face with my hands. How many more uncomfortable revelations could I handle?

"Don't be that way." Rose draped an arm around my shoulders, squeezing tight while touching the side of her head to mine. "My brother is an asshole. We all know this."

"We didn't want to say anything about it because it would hurt your feelings," Valentina explained in a quiet voice. I had always gotten along better with Aria, who was the more empathetic and caring of them. Valentina had always been much more blunt, less patient. To hear her like this came as a surprise.

"Plus, Noah threatened to make our lives miserable if we ever mentioned it." With another squeeze, Rose added, "He felt really bad, and I'm not just saying that because I'm his sister."

My hands dropped away from my face. Nothing about this made sense. "He admitted what he did?"

"He didn't have to. Evan spread the word to us as soon as we got to the dance," Aria explained, gesturing between her and her twin. "He thought it was hysterical, but he was half-drunk by then anyway."

"He sobered up real quick when Noah shoved him up against the wall," Valentina observed, smirking. "I swear, that boy's life flashed before his eyes."

"It was too late by then," Aria concluded. "Evan had already told Pierce. Noah warned him that if he ever said anything to you about it, he could kiss his ass goodbye."

I was still reeling when the twins grinned at each other. "And it didn't suck telling Penny Schwartz we'd get her kicked off the student council for threatening to beat up a freshman." Aria giggled before taking another sip of her mimosa.

They had done all that, and I didn't have clue. All these years, I thought it was our secret. It turned out they had been keeping a secret from me.

"For what it's worth," Rose interjected. "I didn't find out about any of this until after the fact from these two. I wanted so much to go to you, but Noah made me swear not to because it would mean word got out. Nobody wanted to hurt you."

"All because Noah told you to shut up about it?" I concluded. The three of them nodded almost in unison. "That's... surprising."

And he had never said anything to me about it. Why? Why keep it to himself for all these years? Why let me hate him when we could've cleared this up? "I don't understand why he never said anything," I whispered more to myself than to the girls.

It was Rose who provided an answer while pouring herself fresh coffee. "You might have missed the memo, but none of these guys is good at being human. Showing feelings. Apologizing." She rolled her eyes dramatically while we all snickered in recognition of the truth behind her words.

But for ten years?

I couldn't tell myself he'd forgotten about it since my chilly attitude had never warmed up. I had gone through the motions for the sake of our families and friends, but that was where my efforts stopped.

Why couldn't he just apologize and get it over with? No, instead, he had gone out of his way to spare my feelings and threaten to kick some ass.

We changed the subject once Mom came in from

outside, and that worked for me. I was too overwhelmed and conflicted to stay on this topic a minute longer, so I gladly listened to Aria as she complained about the guy from our spin class who'd been giving her major attitude ever since she'd saved a bike for me when he wanted to use it. I couldn't imagine getting mad about something that trivial.

Though I was no stranger to holding a grudge. All those years, I'd hated Noah, resenting him for treating my feelings like they were a joke. Like I was so insignificant, my humiliation didn't matter.

I went through the motions of enjoying our meal, laughing and gossiping the way we could only do without the presence of the guys. As far as I knew, they were out on the Goldsmith family yacht. I wished I could find Noah and pull him aside, though I didn't know what I would say if I had him in front of me. It would probably be best to let the whole thing go. Compared to the mess we were currently in, it seemed inconsequential.

After convincing Mom I'd be fine to drive home, I set off about an hour later. Traffic was light enough that I could cruise at a steady pace, music blaring. I didn't have it in me to sing along like I usually did during a long drive. I barely heard a note, anyway. My mind was too occupied elsewhere.

I was wrong about him.

I was also wrong about me.

I told myself I wouldn't let him get to me, but I had. He was already under my skin before I found out he was the man in the mask who made me do things I'd never dreamed of. And as soon as his hands were on me on Friday night, I didn't have a prayer. There was nothing for me to do afterward but lie there, trying to catch my breath, fighting to figure out what the hell just happened and why I was so disappointed he left before we could continue.

It was hopeless. I would spend the rest of my life torn between craving more of what I had only ever found with him and knowing we could never go anywhere. I wasn't sure I could maintain a casual, hookup-only relationship with him. That wasn't my thing. I had never been able to pull it off.

On top of that, we couldn't keep it a secret for long. It was shocking nobody figured out what happened on Friday, but then they were all busy getting drunk on the beach at the time. I doubt anybody was keeping track of how long Noah was in the house with me. Even if they had, no way would they have guessed what we were up to. Not when I hated him like I did.

Or like I used to.

It was all such a mess, compounded by what I now knew about what went down years back. He had made sure to protect me from the fallout of what he had done. All this time, I had only wanted an apology, but he had done much better. He had wrapped me in a protective bubble to make up for the pain he'd caused.

I had to talk to him.

I needed to clear the air once and for all.

No more assumptions, no more misunderstandings. There was only so much of this push-and-pull I could take.

By the time I pulled into my usual parking spot in my building's garage, I was determined to call him and invite him over. He probably wouldn't get back into town until later in the day, but that would give me time to practice what I wanted to say.

I was out of the car, reaching into the back seat for my bag when another car door opened a few spaces down. I hadn't noticed the Bentley, but I wasn't looking for it. Yet somehow, it made sense to see Noah emerge, hitting me with a hard stare over the top of the car roofs between us.

"What brings you back so early?" I asked with my heart in my throat. The question echoed off the concrete all around us.

"I suddenly remembered some work I had to catch up on." He smirked at what sounded like a lie he'd told as an excuse to get away. "You?"

"Same." I inclined my head toward the elevator doors leading up to my apartment. He nodded, then followed me out of the garage without another word. Like this was how it was meant to be all along.

16

NOAH

Had she ever invited me up to her apartment before? I couldn't remember being here. It was big and airy with minimal decor. I could appreciate that. I didn't like a lot of clutter.

That was hardly at the forefront of my mind on first entering, standing in the foyer once Sienna closed and locked the door behind us. Come to think of it, she hadn't invited me up this time, either. There hadn't been any need to. Some things didn't need to be said, and we had always done so well together without using words.

Now, I could use words. There was no need to pretend we were anyone but who we were. It was a rush, a new level of excitement that compelled me to back her up against the door. She dropped her bag on the floor, her breaths quickening once I pinned her with my body, caging her in with an arm to either side.

"Why did you want me to come up here with you?" I whispered.

"I..." She licked her lips, and I drew a shaky breath while fighting the impulse to claim her then and there.

Not yet.

Not before we had an understanding. There wouldn't be any confusion this time around.

"Don't get all shy on me now. We both know you're not this trembling, timid thing." Lowering my head, my lips brushed her cheek. The back of her head touched the door as she sighed sweetly. "Tell me. What do you want? I want to hear it."

It wasn't that she had a problem admitting what she wanted. It was the fact that she wanted it from me. She couldn't forgive herself for that or justify it after spending a decade hating me.

That was then. Too much had changed. We already knew how good we were together.

"Honestly?" Her voice was weak, breathy. "I was hoping we could talk."

The funny part was I believed her. Still, I took her choice of words into account. "Is that what you're hoping? Now? To talk?" My lips grazed her ear before I ran them down the side of her neck.

Her strained whimper made my dick jump.

"Eventually?" At least she was honest before turning her face toward mine, seeking my kiss. I gave it to her, groaning the way she did when it deepened instantly, our teeth clashing as she crushed her mouth against mine. Her hands ran up my chest, twisting my T-shirt like she wanted to tear it from me.

Fuck, this was different, but in the best way. This time, I knew who she was, and she knew me. I couldn't have predicted how much that would add to the experience.

She groaned in frustration when I broke the kiss. Her nipples were hard enough that I felt them through her top and mine as I rubbed against them, her strained whimpers making my dick throb.

"Here's how this is going to go." Staring deep into her bottomless blue eyes, I grunted out, "You're going to take me to your bedroom. You're going to take off your clothes. You're going to lie back on the bed so I can finally eat that pussy of yours."

She shuddered, melting against me, but said nothing. It didn't matter. I saw the color that flooded her cheeks, the desire swirling in those baby blues.

"And after you come on my tongue, you're going to come on my cock. Are you on the pill?' I asked before we went further.

"Yes," she whispered.

"Good. Now, if you understand these instructions, say yes, Sir." Reaching between us, I cupped her hot mound through her linen slacks. "Do you understand?"

"Yes, Sir," she moaned out when I applied pressure.

"Are you sure? You're not just saying that because you're already dying to come?"

Yes, it was better this way. I got to hear the tremor in her voice, how it went high-pitched and helpless. "I'm sure!"

"Good girl." She stumbled a little when I backed away, but once she adjusted to my absence, she did as instructed, leading me through the living room, the kitchen, and past what looked like a home office. There would be time to look at it later.

I was more interested in staring at her ass, remembering the way it looked after I'd used the crop on it. What a shame I didn't have any of those toys with me, but we could arrange that because this would happen again. We hadn't really started yet, but I already knew that much.

Her room was large, with exposed brick and big

windows overlooking the East River. What interested me more than the view was the four-poster bed, king-sized by the look of it. I instantly envisioned her writhing, wrists tied to two of the posts. Oh, yes, we would have a lot of fun here.

Now, I was on a mission. I needed to eat her while she moaned my name. My heart thudded against my ribs as she began stripping down, untying the drawstring of her pants and allowing them to pool around her ankles before pulling a thin sweater over her head. Her full tits dropped hypnotically once she unhooked her white lace bra and tossed it aside. I couldn't take my eyes off them, already craving her rosy nipples.

Finally, she hooked her thumbs under her thong and lowered it, straightening up quickly and standing in front of me with her arms at her sides. There was no trying to hide herself, no crossing her hands in front of her bald pussy. She was mine, ripe and ready for the taking.

"On the bed. Lie back for me. Spread your legs *wide.*" With no darkness to hide behind, I welcomed the sight of her. I reached down to rub my aching bulge at the sight of her glistening pink folds once her parted thighs revealed them to me.

"So pretty," I sighed, nearly salivating. "Touch yourself. Make sure you're good and wet for me. I want to taste you."

She was barely breathing, slowly sliding her hand down her stomach, and I realized I was holding my breath as her fingers inched closer to her center. When she first dragged a finger through her slit, I released the breath and opened my fly to free my stiff, aching cock.

"Tell me the truth." Stepping up between her spread knees, I watched her fingers dance over her clit. "Did you do this to yourself after we were together? Were you in this bed, touching yourself, thinking of me?"

"Fuck, yes," she breathed out, and I couldn't hide the satisfied smirk. She was only obeying me, holding nothing back.

Sinking to my knees, I lifted her hand and held it close to my nose, breathing her in. "Taste yourself," I growled out, staring as she slid her fingers into her mouth and sucked while I stroked myself to the sight.

It was erotic enough to test my staying power. I could easily have blown my load simply while watching her.

Her back arched at the touch of my tongue to her glistening lips. "Fuck!" She gasped, reaching down, taking the back of my head in her hand. Rather than pull her away, I went with it, letting her almost force me to give her more. To drive my tongue through her folds, lavish long, slow licks against her swollen clit.

And as I did, she whispered, "Oh, God, just like that... feels so good... eat my pussy, Noah..."

Fuck, this was much better than silence. I used her responses to guide me, focusing on what made her squeal, writhe, tug my hair, and grind her hips against my face.

By the time her grinding turned to sharp jerks, my chin was coated in her juices and my cock dripping precum. "Yes! I'm coming! Oh God!"

She released my head to grip the duvet with both fists before going limp with a long, raspy sigh.

More.

I wanted more.

I wanted all of her.

Finally, I could indulge myself in the feel of her, could mold her tits in my palms as I kissed my way up her flat belly. "Fuck, you are perfect," I groaned out, taking one of her nipples into my mouth, then the other, feasting on her while her hands ran over my ass and up my back. She pulled up my shirt, and I released her nipple long enough to let her yank it over my head before going back to work, flicking and sucking, doing anything I could to make her moan my name again. I needed to hear it.

"You are a very good girl." I lapped at her skin, trailing kisses down her body before draping her legs over my shoulders and teasing the silky skin of her thighs. "You came on my tongue just like I told you to. Refresh my memory. What did I say would come next?"

Light flickered in her eyes. "You said I had to come on your cock."

"Such a good listener. Can you do that for me, baby?"

A wicked smile tugged the corners of her mouth. "I always have before." Her eagerness to please me had me stripping down to nothing in no time, as my gaze never left hers. She widened her legs, her glistening pussy on full display. A deep rumble left my throat before cupping the backs of her thighs and dragging her closer. "Oh, yes." Her eyes closed, her head rolling from side to side as I dragged my head through her slit. "So good. Give it to me," she demanded.

"How much do you want it?" I was torturing myself, but I couldn't help it. I needed to hear it.

"I want it so much that I will kill you if you don't give it to me *now*." Her eyes opened partway, finding mine. "Fuck me. I *need* it."

Not what I had in mind, but it worked. Lining up with her hole, I pushed forward, driving myself into her tight sheath.

"Christ," I hissed. The feel of her pussy without anything between us was almost too much to take.

She winced, sucking in a breath through her teeth. "So thick..." she whispered, whimpering as I stretched her. By the time I sank deep, she was panting, her legs hooked around my hips and pressing against my ass.

"More?" I asked, unmoving, watching every twitch of her face as she absorbed the pleasure.

"Fuck yes... Noah... yes..."

I took her like I had before because there was no other choice. I couldn't go slow, not with her beautiful face contorting as the tension built and her muscles tightened. She was already on the verge of another orgasm, and I wanted to give it to her. I wanted to take all day and night and would, if she'd let me.

Her nails sank into my shoulders, dragging them over my skin and bringing a sharp sensation to the forefront of my awareness. My strokes quickened, and soon the bed rocked from the force as I drove her into the mattress. Her pussy tightened, drawing me deeper, a low guttural groan pulling from my throat as I got lost in her.

How many women had I fucked, but something about Sienna made it feel like the first time.

"Yes, fuck me..." she grunted out, teeth gritted, breathing harder.

She was made for me.

Made for this.

She took everything I had and wanted more.

I grazed the shell of her ear with kisses. "Come for me," I whispered, my release threatening to take over. "Come on my cock like a good girl."

"I... I think... I am... fuck!" My ears rang when she screamed, her whole body tightening around mine, legs locked and holding me in place. The rush came over me as soon as her greedy cunt began milking my shaft. I couldn't hold back. I lowered my head, my face against her neck, and came with her.

We stayed that way long after her cries went quiet and turned into heavy breathing, punctuated by a few soft moans of contentment. This was normally the part where I was glad for the experience but ready to move on. I'd blown my load, she was satisfied, and all was well.

It wasn't like that this time. My head swam with confusion when I lifted it, propping myself up on my forearms and looking down at her. She was glowing, wearing a lazy smile—a woman floating in the afterglow sated to her soul.

When her eyes fluttered open and found mine, there was no question in my mind. "That's going to happen again," I announced.

It couldn't be any other way.

"As if you had any choice." Her smile widened as she reached out to run a hand through my hair. "I hope you didn't have any other plans today."

Shit, if she kept talking like that, I'd need to cancel my plans... indefinitely.

17

SIENNA

"We couldn't have picked a more perfect day." The sun was shining brilliantly, and the air was unseasonably warm. That, paired with the fact that it was a Saturday morning, meant the sidewalks were full of pedestrians.

I had to navigate around them while walking a couple of blocks from where I'd parked. Up ahead, I made out a flurry of activity in front of the recreation center, telling me the photographers had already arrived. As far as I knew, the athletes would be there shortly. At least, nobody had sent any messages to the contrary.

"Have fun out there," Jules told me over the phone. "Don't forget to find out if any of those guys are single."

"I've already promised my cousins. Besides, you don't want to date an athlete," I pointed out, stopping at a red light. "So many of them have a girl in every city. I mean, we've been cleaning up their messes for long enough, haven't we?"

"That's true," she agreed with a sigh. "Anyway, if you

happen to spend any time today with whoever you're sleeping with, thank him for me."

The light turned green, but my feet didn't move. Only when somebody bumped into me from behind did I step off the curb. "What are you talking about?" I asked with a high-pitched laugh.

She didn't know.

She couldn't know.

Snorting, she said, "You still think you can fool me. Like I haven't noticed the difference in you this past week."

"Girl, you need a vacation. You're starting to imagine things." It wasn't easy to pretend, but I wasn't about to admit the truth. I'd have to let her think I had a sexy little secret that didn't also involve a complete ethics dilemma. Sleeping with my client, completely aware now of who he was. Before, there was an excuse. I didn't know my mystery man wasn't such a mystery after all.

"Whatever you say. Can't wait to see the photos." We ended the call there, and I released a sigh of relief. Was I being that obvious? Was I normally a shrew or something? Okay, so maybe all the ridiculously hot, amazing sex I'd had with Noah that week had left me with a spring in my step. That was ironic, considering the lack of sleep all that sex had led to, but I wasn't about to complain.

Note to self—stop being so upbeat and happy. I had to laugh at myself as I lifted a hand to wave to one of the photographers who spotted me as I approached. Time to get down to work.

That attitude lasted all of three seconds, approximately the amount of time it took for Noah to emerge from inside the squat cinderblock building. I couldn't have been more shocked if he showed up wearing lingerie. "Look at you!" I called out. "The early bird gets the worm, I guess."

It was not easy pretending there wasn't anything more between us, especially when he looked surprisingly adorable in jeans, a ball cap, and an old-school Yankees jersey. The word *adorable* was not one I ever would have associated with Noah in years past, but things had changed.

I had changed.

He held his arms out to the sides. "Figured I should be in costume." When no one else was looking, he gave me a private, narrow-eyed look. "I barely had time to get home from your place and take a shower. How are you holding up?"

How was I holding up?

My ass was still throbbing slightly from the spanking he gave me last night, a pleasant sensation that reminded me of the fun we had. "This is my second iced latte," I whispered, holding up my plastic cup. There wasn't enough caffeine in existence to make up for the lack of sleep, but I was trying.

At the arrival of a long, sleek bus, we snapped out of our personal chatter. I took the lead, greeting the athletes as they exited the bus, pausing for photos before heading into the building where the kids were waiting. The program's director was inside with them, and I could hear the kids' squeals of excitement before we ever stepped into the lobby and headed for the gymnasium.

I had to make a point to stay away from Noah and hang around on the fringes with parents and family members who'd come out to observe the activities. Otherwise, it would have been too easy to reach out and touch his hand, to touch him in passing.

How had everything changed so quickly? It had only been weeks since I would have sooner eaten broken glass than spend a Saturday with my arch nemesis.

Now, I had to remind myself not to stare at him while he interacted with some of the kids who saw his jersey and assumed he was a baseball player. I covered my mouth with my hand and pretended to cough over a laugh when one of the kids handed him a baseball and asked him to sign it.

But he handled it well, explaining who he was and that he was just as excited to meet these famous players as the kids were. He even sat cross-legged with them on the floor, listening to the program director as he explained how the day would progress. After that, it was time to head outside. If the weather had been bad, we would've stayed inside, and I thanked my lucky stars we wouldn't be closed in with a bunch of screaming, excited kids all day.

I liked kids a lot, but put a few dozen of them in an enclosed space where their sneakers could squeak nonstop while they shrieked for hours—no, thank you.

Besides, I had other work to do. There was no reason for me to participate in any of the activities, and I had expected to clear out my email inbox and review a few status reports from my team while the kids learned how to swing a bat and throw a football.

What I didn't factor in was how intriguing Noah's interactions with the kids would be. I'd imagined he would hang back and offer a few tight smiles to the photographers to make everything look legit. I didn't think he would actually participate, playing catch with a few of the kids, even helping to wrangle them when they got a little too rambunctious. Was this who he'd been all along, and I was only now noticing? I had let go of my preconceived notions, giving him plenty of space to surprise the hell out of me.

Or he could simply have gone out of his way to impress me. It didn't matter, did it? The outcome was the same, either way. There were a lot of happy kids and plenty of photos we could plaster all over the internet.

He would make a good dad someday.

Whoa, hold up.

I was almost disappointed in myself for letting that thought leak through. The man tossed a ball back and forth with a few kids, and suddenly, I was imagining him with kids of his own. I was too smart to fool myself like that, wasn't I? Didn't I know better?

It didn't matter. Not when the sound of his lighthearted laughter was music to my ears. I had never seen him this way or known he had it in him to be so sweet and patient. He even noticed when one of the kid's shoes came untied and tied it for him before he could trip and hurt himself.

Be still my quivering ovaries.

By the time lunch rolled around, I hadn't gotten a bit of work done, and I didn't care. I was actually enjoying myself, laughing and applauding, chatting with a few of the parents who'd been able to come out with the kids. While I did, I glanced over toward where Noah was receiving instruction from a quarterback on how to throw the perfect spiral. Our eyes met, and he grinned, and oh, my heart.

I was in a lot of trouble.

It would never work. I knew that. We were having fun, that was all. It would be hopelessly cliché for us to try to make it anything else, especially when everyone in our lives would have strong, loud opinions about us being together— a relationship with my brother's best friend.

This wasn't a sitcom.

Though at the same time, Rose and Colton were happy, weren't they? So happy they almost set my teeth on edge, living in a blissful little bubble. Maybe it was possible.

But this was Noah, and he didn't do relationships. He

would get bored of me. I would be the world's biggest idiot if I walked into this with eyes wide open, knowing him the way I did, not expecting to end up with a bruised heart.

Even so, it was a fun morning. And once the kids settled down with their lunches, I approached him while looking as serious as I could. "Can I talk to you for a minute?" I asked, nodding in acknowledgment of the guys he was chatting with. "You can talk about buying a team later," I added, winking. He rolled his eyes with a good-natured groan before following me out of the gym where the food had been set up. I led him to the front lobby before ducking into a little alcove where opposite doors marked the restrooms.

"What's up?" he murmured a second before I took his hand and pulled him into the empty girls' room with me.

"This." Standing on my tiptoes, I took him by the back of the neck and pulled him down until our mouths met. I'd been craving his kiss for hours, I realized, and I indulged in the taste of him, his smell, and the soft growl that rumbled in his throat before his arms encircled my waist so he could pull me tight against him. There was something to be said for having a sexy little secret, and by the time his dick pressed urgently against my hip, I was hot and wet.

"What are you doing?" He laughed softly as I crouched in front of him while gazing up into his eyes, working his belt and dipping a hand inside his fly to withdraw his gorgeous, erect dick.

I didn't say a word. What was the point of speaking when the act of wrapping my lips around his shaft said all I needed anyway? He closed his eyes, his head falling back against the tiled wall.

Before long, I was slurping on him, my head bobbing, cheeks hollowing out. We didn't have much time, and this was risky enough as it was. That only added to the thrill, my heart racing, wetness pooling in my panties while his breathing went faster, sharper, one hand against the back of my head.

He fisted my hair beneath his fingers and started to thrust into my mouth, but I was in control, not him. He wasn't calling the shots this time.

I sucked even harder, moaning around the base of his cock as my tongue ran along the ridge. His grip tightened in my hair, and his breath caught when a rush of warmth filled my mouth, followed by a raspy hiss. I swallowed greedily, taking every drop. By the time he started to soften in my mouth, his legs were shaking. "Holy shit," he whispered, laughing softly, and his breathlessness left me grinning smugly as I stood. "What did I do to deserve that?"

I wouldn't have told him in a million years how ridiculously hot it was watching him out there. How much it made me want him more than I ever had. Instead, I settled for a coy smile before rinsing my mouth at the sink. "Let's say that's a reward for playing along today."

I glanced up at the mirror in time to see his smile. "It's not so bad," he admitted. "I'm kind of enjoying it." An understatement, but I wouldn't challenge him on it. If he knew how clear it was that he was having a good time, it might have spoiled everything.

"We'd better get back out there before we're missed." As it was, I heard a couple of the little boys excitedly talking as they entered the men's room across from where we stood. Lunch would be wrapping up soon. I pulled the door open a crack and peered out to make sure the coast was clear. There were a handful of offices across from the restrooms, but the lights were off behind the windows looking out over the lobby. We were safe.

"Let's go." Taking his hand, I pulled him along behind me, only letting go once we were out in the hall again.

"Remind me to return the favor later," he told me in a soft voice before we parted ways.

As if I wouldn't.

As if he would need to be reminded.

18

NOAH

"Noah."

Nobody had ever whispered my name like she did, and nobody ever would. It was already close to dawn, and the light filtering through the windows painted her naked body, letting me admire the sight of her riding me.

She braced herself against my chest with both hands, eyes closed, mouth hanging open. I'd never been with anyone who lost themselves as completely as she did. There were no inhibitions, no self-consciousness. She wasn't afraid to go after what she wanted.

At the moment, what she wanted was to come on my cock.

I looked down between us, watching my glistening shaft disappear inside her tightening pussy. Her tits swayed gently with each stroke. I teased her nipples, and she moaned, grinding hard against my pelvis.

"Do you have one more in you?" I whispered. I had lost count of the times she'd come, the two of us only stopping to doze off now and then before starting again.

I couldn't get enough of her. The fact that she felt the same was beyond gratifying. There was something profound about it, the way we connected. The way I craved her night and day.

We'd come back here on Saturday afternoon, and she had yet to leave. I couldn't let her go.

"I... Noah... I'm going to come..." she whined, her pace quickening as she rode me harder, throwing her silky hair back in those last moments. I managed to wait until she cried out and fell against me, and those tiny muscles began to milk me dry.

Closing my eyes, I gave myself over to it, filling her, savoring the broken cries barely audible over the roaring in my ears. I was too wiped out to speak or do much of anything but stroke her hair as she shuddered and moaned in the aftermath, draped across my chest.

"Oh, God," she whispered. "I keep thinking it can't get better, and then it does. I think I'm developing a habit."

I already knew I'd developed one. In moments like this, it was easy to imagine this becoming the norm. No matter what happened out there in the so-called real world, we would have this to come back to. A sense of peace came over me, complete contentment, and I drifted back to sleep with her in my arms and a smile on my face.

By the time I woke with a start, the faint, gray light had turned to sunshine that spilled across the bedroom. My mouth was dry and my vision blurry. I realized my phone had woken me, still ringing as I fumbled for it on the night-stand. Sienna rolled away, muttering, still half asleep.

Dad. *Shit.* Only he would call at six thirty on Monday morning and expect me to answer. Considering I could already hear his shitty attitude in my head, it seemed a good idea to pick up. I did my best to sound awake when I did. "Hello?"

He wasted no time. "What the hell do you think you're doing?"

Any residual drowsiness evaporated at the sound of his snarling. This was hardly the first time I had been greeted that way by the man. Rose had always been his favorite. Nobody had to tell me that. I had known for years, ever since she first showed interest in the family business. She was his shining star, the apple of his eye and all that shit. I was the black sheep who didn't feel like following in his footsteps.

"Good morning to you too." I sat up, scrubbing a hand over my face.

"Sure. Play dumb. That's what you do best. I was pulling for you, Noah. How could you throw everything away?"

He was serious. I turned my head, looking over my shoulder at Sienna. She rubbed her eyes, frowning at what must've been dread etched across my face. No doubt she could hear him. He was shouting, almost screaming.

And he was on a roll. "Tell me why. Why couldn't you have been smart this time? Do you realize I've already gotten a call from Barrett? Your mother's beside herself."

"Okay, back up. What are you talking about?" This time, Sienna's phone rang, and she scrambled to grab it before hurrying from the room. Normally, the sight of her bare ass would have left me staring after her like a slobbering dog, but I could barely pay attention with Dad shouting in my ear.

"Of course, I should've known better than to think you would be up and reading the news at this time of day." The phone buzzed in my hand. "I texted you the article with the photos. Explain yourself."

It wasn't an article but more like a few lines of shitty text accompanying a series of images that made my stomach drop.

Images of Sienna and me, emerging hand-in-hand from the bathroom at the rec center two days ago, her peering out to make sure we were alone, and my goofy, stupid grins as she led me out. Where the fuck was the person who took it? I couldn't remember seeing anybody. Had they been hiding in one of the offices, waiting for us?

"Well?" Dad demanded, still on speakerphone, while I stared in horror at what was in front of me. It was impossible. How the fuck did it happen? "There have been many times when I've asked myself if you were too spoiled. I've asked myself when you were going to get serious. Building a business is one thing, yet you've always had a penchant for poor decision-making. But this? You've outdone yourself this time."

I forced my way through his disgust. "Dad, I'm telling you—"

"I don't remember asking you to tell me a damn thing," he snapped. There was so much bitterness in his voice, so much anger. "No, you listen to me. It is one thing for you to fuck around with your own life, but when you start interfering with others, I have to step in. You owe a lot of people an apology for this. How do you think this is going to look to the public? You can't keep your dick in your pants long enough to clear up your reputation."

I had no way to defend myself because there was no defense I could offer. I had been caught red-handed. There was no denying what was going on between Sienna and me. The looks on our faces said it all. We were a couple who had sneaked off for a little fun when we were only supposed to be working together, and now any credibility I might have gained would be flushed down the toilet.

That was nothing compared to the way my heart seized for her. "I have to work this out," I told my father, who only snickered like he didn't believe me before I ended the call and threw the phone onto the bed.

Fuck.

In the blink of an eye, everything had gotten so much worse.

Sienna stumbled in a moment later, nose red, eyes swollen and watery. I was in the middle of leaving a voicemail for Maxim. "I swear to God..." I told him. "We'll work this out. Call me as soon as you get this. We can run damage control ASAP." As I spoke, my phone buzzed with an incoming text. I pulled the phone from my ear to read it.

Colton: *Are you fucking kidding me with this? You goddamn hypocrite.*

Son of a bitch!

Things were falling apart in record time, and all I could do was stand back and watch it happen. What else was there to do? Word was spreading, and before long, the world would know I was fucking the woman tasked with cleaning up my image.

But it was still Sienna I was most worried about, who sat on the edge of my bed with her face in her hands, her shoulders shaking. "Jules said she couldn't work with anybody she can't trust." She sobbed. "My mom left a voicemail, and she was crying and so embarrassed. How could I have been so stupid?"

"We're going to get to the bottom of this." I got up, pulling on a pair of sweatpants I'd left on the floor last night.

"Do you think so?" She lowered her hands and looked

up at me, searching my face, clearly desperate to believe what I said.

I had done this to her. She would never have taken a risk like that if it wasn't for me. Now, her business partner was ready to walk, and she would probably lose credibility with her employees and clients.

"No. You're right." She ran her hands over her cheeks, nodding firmly. Following my lead, she got up and searched for her clothes, which had been discarded at random as I peeled them off her. "This is fine. There is nothing I can't figure out. It'll just take a little work, that's all."

My fault.

All my fault.

Now she ran around like a chicken with her head cut off, rambling about strategy and covering her ass while her bare feet slapped the hardwood. "Sienna," I murmured, watching her.

Either she couldn't hear me over her own voice, or she didn't want to. "And honestly, what do a few grainy pictures prove? Unless somebody actually witnessed what was going on, it's all speculation and ugly headlines. Who the hell would have done this? What's in it for them? This is what we need to find out."

"Sienna." I took her by the shoulders as she tried to hurry past me, holding her in place. "Stop for a second. Listen to me."

"There's no time! I have to go try to talk some sense to Jules. She's losing it, and it's all my fault." Her voice cracked before she began trembling in my grip.

"It's not your fault," I told her, my heart heavy. "It's mine. I got you into this. It's obvious we made a mistake."

Finally, she heard me. I'd gotten through to her. "What

are you saying?" she whispered as her flushed face went pale. "No, this isn't the time for that."

"If it isn't, then when? Here's what we're going to do." Fuck, this was the last thing I wanted, and putting it into words took everything I had. "You're going to tell everybody it was a one-time thing, a mistake, and that it won't happen again."

"Wait a second."

"And then, we're going to put that into practice because we have both worked too hard to throw everything away by looking like a couple of thoughtless, horny kids." As I spoke, her face fell, but the truth in my words didn't change. Nothing changed. I would've rather cut out my own tongue than admit it out loud, but my father was right. I couldn't be irresponsible, not now. There was much too much riding on this.

Why was there so much hope in her eyes as they searched mine? Why couldn't she accept this? "You know I'm right," I insisted. It was the hardest thing I'd ever done, letting go of her, but I forced myself through it. For her sake, if not for my own. I wouldn't drag her down with me, and she was too big a temptation to resist.

I released her and backed away, turning toward the bathroom. "I've got to shower, then try to track down Maxim. Everything's going to be fine. You handle what you need to, and I'll take care of things on this end."

She didn't move, rooted to the spot in the center of my bedroom. "So that's it?"

"It has to be. It's a shame it had to turn out this way," I added as her eyes went watery again. "At least we can't say we didn't enjoy ourselves."

I didn't believe myself. I heard the emptiness behind my words, but it changed nothing. This was how it had to be. I had worked too hard to throw it all away, even for somebody like Sienna. And she had worked too hard to throw her life away on me. I had done some regrettable shit in my time, but to ruin her would be unforgivable.

She let out a single, faint whimper before finding her purse and fishing a pair of large sunglasses from inside. Sliding them on did little to disguise the fact that she'd been crying. With a long, shuddery breath, she squared her shoulders, lifted her chin, and walked out to the front door while I watched.

I was watching her walk out of my life. No, that wasn't true. She would always be part of my life, an ever-present reminder of my stupid weakness and my ability to ruin the lives of the people around me. I would never be rid of her.

And even now, full of regret and self-loathing, I knew I didn't want to forget.

I didn't want to forget a minute of it.

19

SIENNA

This was new, feeling like I had to tiptoe around my own company on Tuesday morning after spending Monday wandering my apartment like a zombie, hiding from the world. I was the first person to arrive, hell-bent on doing damage control inside and outside the business. Jules had sent out a call to get everybody in and at their desks as early as they could manage this morning. All hands on deck.

And all because of me.

Beating myself up wouldn't help anything, but at the moment, it was all I could do. Stupid, so stupid, what was I thinking? That had not been the time or the place to go down on him, but I had done it anyway. I knew better than that. It was my job to know better.

It didn't matter. Now, I could only try to make it up to the people I had inadvertently hurt. First on the list was my business partner, who barely looked at me as she took a seat in my office without stopping at her desk first to remove her jacket or leave her purse. That might have been the toughest part of all, the way she refused to meet my gaze.

"I've been doing some digging," I told her while she arranged herself in the chair across from mine. "You know, Noah has been convinced all along that it was Drake Thomas behind that article. But after going through his social media posts this morning, I'm inclined to believe it wasn't him."

She tipped her head to the side, eyes narrowing as she regarded me the way she would regard a suspicious stranger. Was this how far we had fallen? "What has that got to do with anything?" she asked.

"I'm operating under the assumption that whoever took and shared these photos is the same person trying to take Noah down. Drake is out of the country."

"I see." She didn't say anything more than that. I had no way of knowing what was going on in her head.

I had done this to myself, right? A chilly attitude was the least of what I deserved.

"I sent a request to the photographers yesterday. They sent the photos from the clinic over to me. I've been combing through them all morning, but I haven't found anything necessarily suspicious."

"Okay, can we drop this for a second?" She tucked her chin close to her chest, her brows raised. "How could you do this? You, of all people. You're supposed to be the one person I can trust because we've both sacrificed so much for this company."

"I know, and I am so sorry." If anything, I was glad she had brought it up since there was no ignoring the elephant in the room. It took up all the space and the oxygen. "It was stupid, and I have no excuse. I don't blame you if you never forgive me, but please, let's not throw *everything* away."

"I wouldn't be the one throwing it away," she countered, almost slamming her iced coffee on my desk. "It would be *you*. You are the one who did this. All I can do now is deal with the fallout. Do you understand how much credibility we've lost?"

"Do you have any idea how much I've beaten myself up because of that?" I countered in a fierce whisper. "Yes, I'm completely aware. And *I am* sorry. I wish I could go back and do it differently, but I can't. All I can do is try to clean up the mess. And I am trying, I really am."

"I know you are." *But it doesn't make a difference.* She didn't have to say it. I felt it, and it hurt. It made me wonder if we could ever get back to where we started. Back when she trusted me.

"Was it worth it?" she whispered. Her voice was shaking, and tears were in her eyes when she finally bothered meeting my gaze.

"It's so much more complicated than that." Normally, that would be her cue to wave it off and tell me not to bother, that she wasn't going to pry. Except, she didn't do that. She merely settled back in the chair, coffee in hand again, wearing an expectant look.

I had already swallowed my pride so many times. Why not once more? "You're the only person who knows this," I warned before launching into the story of how I had accidentally ended up getting involved with Noah. She didn't need the details, of course, so I left them out. It was enough to explain how it all started out accidentally, thanks to her invitation to the party at Club Caramel.

Her mouth hung open by the time I finished. Somewhere along the line, she had gone from sitting back with her arms folded to leaning in, hanging on to every word. "And it was him all along? Holy shit. What are the chances?"

"Believe me. You're not asking yourself anything I

haven't already asked myself a hundred times, and I still haven't figured it out." There was something refreshing about coming clean. I felt lighter, having unburdened myself.

"That doesn't absolve you," she pointed out, though she was no longer as chilly and detached. "You know that, right?"

"Of course it doesn't. I was stupid to sneak off with him on Saturday. And I'm so sorry to bring any of this down on us. It's going to be all right," I insisted.

She didn't look convinced. "I guess you won't want to hear about the call I got from Jacob Dalton first thing this morning, or rather, from his agent." She was angry again, nostrils flaring with every breath. "He asked me point-blank if Jacob could get out of the contract because they aren't sure we're the right fit."

"That son of a bitch!" I slammed a hand against my desk because out of everything, that was the straw that broke the camel's back. "He fucking hits on me at lunch, then has the nerve to act like he can't believe I get involved with a client?"

"Maybe that's exactly why he did it," she pointed out, sounding tired. "If you were going to abandon your ethics, you should've abandoned them with him. You know how these things go down." At least there was sympathy in her voice.

"I'm sorry. I am *so, so* sorry," I mumbled, folding my arms on the desk and resting my head on top. "I will never stop hating myself for this."

She kept me hanging for a moment or two before sighing. "I don't want you to hate yourself forever. We'll get through this. I know we will. It's just... a lot."

That was putting it mildly. She sounded less like she

wanted to kill me, anyway, which was a huge relief. I could hold onto that.

"I'm going to go out there to see if anybody has any questions or concerns."

No, don't worry about it," she insisted when I began to rise from my chair. "Keep combing through those photos. Maybe send them over to Noah. He might be able to recognize somebody you would otherwise overlook."

It wasn't that I hadn't considered that yet. I had already run through countless options in my head. For twenty-four hours, I had worried myself sick, answering phone calls from my parents, from Rose, the twins. There was a point when I wanted to throw my hands into the air and give up, to tell everybody to check in with each other rather than bothering me. But I was an adult, and as such, I had to face the music.

That didn't mean, however, that I wanted to reach out to Noah. It wasn't exactly like he had kicked me out of his penthouse, but that didn't make the aftermath any easier to swallow. I had heard Ari. At least I had heard how angry he was, even if I couldn't make out the exact words he used before Jules called me in a panic after seeing the photos online. I was sure when he looked at me, he saw the origin of all of his troubles. He had taken a huge risk with me, and it had blown up in our faces. And now, all the work we had done to clear up his image may as well have never happened.

That was how it felt, anyway. Time would tell if it was true. In the meantime, there was nothing I could do but put on my big girl panties and type up an email to him.

Got some photos from the sports clinic. Thought maybe you could recognize somebody who might have taken those shots of us...

That didn't feel like enough. What could I say? Should I thank him? No, that would come off so corny, not to mention a little patronizing. *Thanks for the best sex ever.* Yeah, that would make everything better. What was I thinking?

... I hope things have calmed down a little from yesterday. Let me know if there's anything I can do.

Sienna Black

CEO

Momentum Public Relations

I sent the message before I could overthink it any further, then resolved to step out of my office for the first time since my arrival. I needed to face the team. I needed to be a leader, no matter how much I wanted to crawl under a blanket and never come back out.

I stood, straightening out my suit jacket, smoothing down any errant flyaways before stepping away from my desk, only to be halted by my ringing phone. Even now, my heart leaped when I saw Noah's name on the screen. Was I trying to have my heart broken? I took a single, shaky breath before answering. "Don't tell me you already saw somebody in those photos."

There was a brief pause before he replied. "I haven't opened the file yet. I wanted to talk to you. Yesterday went all wrong."

I squeezed my eyes shut. No, I couldn't do this. There was no giving in. No working things out. "It went the way it had to. We're both adults with big responsibilities. You were right."

"What about everything else?"

"There is no everything else," I reminded him as gently as I could while my heart twisted and burned. This was so fucking unfair, but then life wasn't fair. "We both worked too hard and too long to be irresponsible now. I think all of this can be handled and cleaned up, but that doesn't mean we can pretend none of it happened and go back to how things were before those photos came out."

"Can we at least talk?" he asked, quiet, hesitant.

So unlike the Noah I thought I knew.

So unlike the Noah who'd broken my heart all over again by letting me down gently yesterday morning.

I looked out the window at the view I loved so much, willing myself to get through this without breaking down. "We're talking now." He was determined to kill me, wasn't he? How many times had I wished he would regret hurting me? How many times did I imagine him at my mercy, begging for a chance to be understood, asking for my forgiveness? Reality wasn't nearly as satisfying as my fantasies, but then a lot of water had passed under the bridge since then.

"I have to go," I told him, biting my lip, fighting through the regret that threatened to steal my voice. "I need to do a little damage control around the office. Do yourself a favor and look through the photos. Drake Thomas is out of the country," I added. "So I doubt he was behind this."

"All right." Disappointment hung heavy in his voice, but that wasn't my problem. I couldn't manage the way he dealt with this. I could only manage myself.

And I was having a hard enough time of that without taking on the burden of his feelings. I was having such a hard time, in fact, that it took a few minutes to catch my breath after ending the call. There was something terribly final about it, and painful too. Somewhere along the line, I had gotten much too involved with him, so much so, there were tears threatening to spill onto my cheeks when I imagined never touching him again.

But it was for the best. One of us had to be smart about this, and it looked like it was going to be me. No matter how much misery I'd have to wade through to get to the other side.

20

NOAH

The last thing I expected when Maxim burst into my office on Tuesday morning was to find him smiling. I'd been waiting for him to storm in, tell me all the various ways I could fuck myself, then announce he was dissolving our partnership. After spending Sunday and Monday ducking me, he could've been up to anything. Interviewing lawyers, for starters.

Instead, he beamed from ear to ear, tossing a folder on my desk. "It's official. We got our guy, and all because you forwarded those photos to me. You're welcome," he concluded.

"Are you serious?" I grabbed for the folder the way I would grab for a life preserver in open water. Sending Maxim the photos had been a last-ditch effort to get him to respond. Pitiful, yes, but it seemed to have worked.

"I called up a friend of mine who works in law enforcement. Don't ask for specifics," he quickly warned, scowling when I glanced up from the images in the folder. Dropping into a chair in front of the desk, he continued, "I had him run the photos from the event through some kind of software they use to identify suspects at large, then ran that against our employee ID photos. There was a match. Luke Washington. He's one of our property managers."

"Slow down." Sure enough, the printed photos were from the rec center, and I recognized the same man in all of them—medium height, average build, somebody who could easily melt into the background no matter where he happened to be. On Saturday, he'd stood off to the side, alone, while most of the other bystanders stood in clusters.

"I pulled his personnel file," Maxim announced. "He's unmarried, no children, and lives in Jersey City."

"There was no reason for him to be there," I murmured, trying to put it all together. "Why was he there?"

"He's sitting at his desk at this very minute if you'd like to ask him." Maxim held up a finger, almost like he'd forgotten something. "Oh, did I mention he's friends on Facebook with a handful of journalists? And he reposted the article about you several times across a handful of platforms."

"Seems a little odd for somebody to spread ugly gossip about their boss unless they have an ax to grind," I mused, sliding the photos away from me. I had seen enough of the snake who quite possibly had gone out of his way to tank my career.

"I was considering pulling him into my office and grilling the shit out of him, but..." he smirked, "... would you like to do the honors?"

"What the hell do you think?" I would knife anybody who tried to get between me and the pleasure of firing this prick. First, I would need to hear his explanation—if he had one.

Maxim stood and buttoned his suit jacket before crossing my office and opening the door. From where I sat, I could see him striding down the hall. The confusion and resentment that had festered for weeks began to crystalize now that I had somewhere to direct it.

There he was, trailing behind Maxim. I hadn't noticed him at the clinic. Fuck, we could've had a full conversation, and I wouldn't have made the connection. I couldn't possibly know all my employees' faces and names.

I wouldn't soon forget his, though. He had the nerve to stride in like he owned the place, smiling like nothing out of the ordinary was happening. Was he oblivious, or did he honestly believe he had gotten away with his bullshit?

Maxim perched on the corner of my desk, facing Luke once he came to a stop in front of me. The guy did a decent job of looking pleasant, which was what confirmed my suspicions. He didn't look nervous about being called into the CEO's office for the first time.

"Luke." The name threatened to curdle in my mouth. "I understand you were at the rec center in the Bronx on Saturday. I must have missed you."

"The Bronx?" He was not a skilled liar, that was for sure. His pathetic attempt at stalling was the sort of thing I did back when I was trying to get out of being punished for staying out all night or denting up my car. Kid stuff.

"Yes, the Bronx. Where I was participating in a sports clinic for kids."

"An event whose details were posted online by the PR company," Maxim added in a low voice.

"Drop the act," I warned when Luke offered a weak shrug. "The photographers caught you more than once. You had no reason to be there. You don't have kids, no nieces or nephews, you don't even live in the neighborhood. Tell me. Why were you there?"

He turned his wide-eyed gaze onto Maxim like he was waiting for clarification, but Maxim wouldn't give an inch.

"Go ahead," he muttered, inclining his head in my direction. "Mr. Goldsmith asked you a question."

Luke's gaze bounced between us, his throat working when he gulped. "I... I mean... it seemed like an interesting day, something I wanted to be a part of."

"You didn't participate," I pointed out as my blood pressure climbed. "I would've remembered that."

"You mean you enjoy attending events where you know there will be dozens of kids running around?" Maxim snickered, shaking his head. "You might want to come up with a better excuse because that sounds a little sketchy. If we brought in the police and had them seize your phone, would there be photos of little kids all over it?"

I folded my arms. "Or would there be photos of *me?*"

Luke's shoulders slumped. He knew we had him. "What else was I supposed to do?" he murmured, the energy having drained from his voice. "You ruined my sister's life. You destroyed my family."

What a sudden left turn. I was damn close to getting whiplash. "How did I do that?" I gritted out. "I don't know your sister."

"Danielle Stevenson. Doesn't ring a bell?" When I lifted a shoulder, he laughed bitterly. "No, I guess it wouldn't. Not with all the women you run through like Kleenex. Let me refresh your memory. I brought her to the holiday party last year when my girlfriend got sick. Dani needed a night out, and I wanted to impress her a little, I guess. Ringing any bells yet?"

Last year's holiday party. How was I supposed to remember that? "You're saying I slept with your sister?"

His lip curled in a snarl. "I'm saying you slept with my sister, her husband found out, and he left her. She had nothing. She went into a deep depression, wound up... sick." His voice broke, but he pushed past it. "She ended up having to live with our parents again because we're afraid of what she'll do to herself if she's left alone. And that's on you."

"I'm sorry about what happened to your sister," I told him, choosing my words carefully. "But I don't sleep with married women. That's a line I don't cross. She must've taken off her ring."

"Besides..." Maxim interjected. "That wouldn't be Mr. Goldsmith's fault. She made a decision, and it's unfortunate how things turned out. Is that why you orchestrated that article?"

It was a gamble. We didn't know he was behind the article. Even his presence at the rec center didn't mean he was the culprit behind the photos.

Except it paid off.

"Not his fault? I should've known you'd take his side!" He was shaking, red-faced, sweat now trickling down the sides of his thin face. "Guys like you think you can get away with it. Whatever you want! You throw some money at a problem, and it's done. You meet a woman, you fuck her, you abandon her, and forget she exists. What's it matter? You'll just find somebody new, right? Who cares about what happens to them?"

"Which is why you tried to destroy my reputation." My fists tightened, hidden from view by my desk. "To get back at me."

"Hell yes, that's why." Lifting his chin, he added, "I did it for Dani."

What a fucking hero. "So you would've destroyed the company that employed you and your coworkers to get back at me for something I didn't know had happened and couldn't have changed anyway?"

Realization dawned upon the prick, but it was too

fucking late.

"Security will escort you from the building," I announced as Maxim went to the door and waved someone inside. "Once you've taken your personal items from your desk, you'll turn over any keys to the properties you manage before you leave."

"You fucking bastard." Luke snarled, but it was too late for that. Hell, I might have respected him more if he'd been a man about it and dealt with this face-to-face. He was still arguing, shouting, and shaking as two guards came in at Maxim's signal and took him from the room.

There was a lot of hushed whispering and shocked exclamations out there. I released a deep breath, sinking against the back of my chair.

"Imagine that." Maxim shook his head as he watched things unfold from my doorway. "Trying to tank your life and the whole company all because his sister decided to cheat on her husband with you."

"He needed somebody to blame," I muttered. "It's over now."

The truth behind my words hit me like a cannonball. It was all over. Luke had done me a favor in the long run. He had given me a reason to go to that party at Club Caramel to find Sienna there and connect with her. He had also driven us apart, following me to that rec center, selling those photos to the tabloids. He had brought an end to what he had started. It was all over.

I didn't know where to go next. I didn't know anyone who could show me a direction to go in.

Or did I? There was one person who wouldn't bullshit me because he never had. Considering I couldn't talk to my best friend about his sister, there was only one other man to turn to.

Picking up my phone, I reluctantly sent Dad a text.
Me: *Can you meet for a drink at five?*

"It's not that you got involved with Sienna." My father sipped his scotch, wearing a thoughtful expression. "That's not what everyone got so upset about. I can speak for your mother when I tell you that."

The bar was still fairly quiet this early in the evening, which was not something I would complain about. Pouring my guts out to my dad was enough of a pain in the ass without worrying about witnesses. "What is it? Because I need to make things right with a lot of people. Now that I have this work issue put behind me, I can deal with my personal life."

"It was the sneakiness behind it, for one thing. The fact that you were supposed to be working together to save your reputation and company, but you ended up doing the very thing that got you into trouble in the first place. One day, when you have your own kids, you'll understand what it's like to be a parent standing on the sidelines, watching your son do precisely the wrong thing. It's difficult for a parent to sit back and witness that."

I could see where he was coming from as I stared into my glass, mulling it over. "Neither of us intended for it to happen," I admitted. It wasn't easy opening up to my father this way. While we didn't have the sort of contentious relationship Colton used to have with Barrett, we weren't exactly warm. I wasn't Rose.

"For what it's worth..." he said. "Sienna could do much worse, and you sure as hell could do worse than Sienna," he added, rolling his eyes. "God knows."

"Well, that's over now. I'll have to patch up my reputation on my own while she does the same for herself since I ruined it."

"Haven't you figured out by now that people have very short memories? I'd bet the cabin in Vail that if Sienna had her team publish a story about one of your employees going out of his way to ruin you, this would all be wrapped up with no problem."

A tempting idea, for sure, but... "It's better if we don't have anything to do with each other now." I went out of my way to avoid his penetrative stare.

"Would you mind a little advice from someone older and wiser?" I eyed him warily but nodded. How much worse could it get? He angled his body on the barstool until he faced me straight-on. Aside from the lines at the corners of his eyes and the silver running through his dark hair, I could've been looking in a mirror. "I respect everything you did to clear up your image, and I'm sure the money you donated to all those causes will do a lot of good for a lot of people. If nothing else, you've got that to hang onto."

"Why do I feel like there's a but hanging in the air?"

His lips twitched before he shrugged. "But there's another way to go about this. I wonder if you've considered it."

"What would that be? I'm all ears."

Shrugging, he said, "Come clean. Tell the truth."

"I'm not trying to hide anything from anyone."

Arching an eyebrow, he countered, "Are you sure? Because from what I can tell, all you've done so far is bend over backward to change public perception. Why not come out and say yes, I know I fucked up? Yes, I'm a human being like anyone else. Before you can tell me you aren't..." he added with a growl. "I'm here to tell you you're wrong. You're just like anybody else. Just as vulnerable to mistakes. And if it was a mistake, being with Sienna, come out and admit it. That's all you have to do. No more lies, no more trying to bend public perception to your will."

"If only it were that simple." I finished what was left in my glass and placed it on the bar with a thump. Funny, the way it brought to mind the banging of a gavel.

"It doesn't have to be difficult," he pointed out. "Come clean. Own up to your mistakes. That's what a man does."

The problem was I didn't see Sienna as a mistake. What we had was not a mistake. How could it be when it hurt so fucking bad to be without her? I couldn't shrug this off and pretend it was all a matter of an intense physical connection, a chemistry I had become addicted to indulging in. I wouldn't be that blasé about it now. Too much had changed. It wasn't her body I missed. I did miss it, of course, but I missed *her* more.

Her shrewd intelligence, her knack for calling me on my bullshit, her sense of humor. I wasn't afraid to be seen, to be known by her. Life was pale and sad without her in it. Even my work, which not long ago had been the focal point of my existence, didn't carry the same weight. Striving for my first billion? It was a goal, but the meaning behind it was gone if there was ever a meaning in the first place.

Dad waited for me to think this through before clapping a hand over my shoulder. "Listen. If you could build a nearly billion-dollar business from the ground up before you've hit thirty, you can do this. I have faith in you."

Of all times for him to tell me that. "You're right," I decided, bolstered by his long-overdue praise. All I had to do was figure out how to make it work.

If I couldn't make things right with the woman I suspected I loved, what was the point of anything?

21

SIENNA

"This is exactly what I needed. I'm just glad you let me take your place." Stretching out my legs in front of me, I admired the jet's interior for the hundredth time since takeoff. "Are you sure you don't hate me for touring the resort instead of you?"

Jules coughed loudly into the phone. Technology was incredible. I could hear her as clearly as if she were sitting on the jet with me, though I was already thousands of miles away. "It's not your fault, babe. It's this damn flu bug. At least one of us can go out there and review the resort."

I spent a lot of time handholding and babysitting fragile clients, but opportunities like this one offset the teeth-grinding I did most days of the week. A client of ours was opening a new resort in the Maldives, which happened to be one of my favorite vacation places in the entire world. We would recommend the resort to our other clients, encourage them to visit and spread the word to their friends, meaning more publicity.

The company had sent a private jet to fly me out there, and I sat back with champagne roughly halfway through the flight. One day, maybe once I was my parents' age, I would take more time for this kind of thing and enjoying the fruits of all my labor.

First, I'd have to hold onto my company, though things were looking good. A few prospects who'd seemed eager to sign on with us had suddenly changed their minds in the days since the tabloid photos were published, but our faithful, satisfied base seemed happy to stick around. Nobody could argue with our results.

"Have fun, test all the amenities, and try not to get a wicked sunburn," Jules advised. I promised I would do my best before ending the call to watch a movie. There was plenty of time to kill.

And I needed the distraction.

I couldn't get a grip on my brain anymore. I couldn't discipline myself enough to keep my thoughts from drifting to Noah at the most inconvenient times.

An entire week had passed without hearing from him, though his CFO had reached out to let us know they found their culprit. The issue with the photos in the tabloids had blown over, thanks to a flurry of activity on our end. We had gone full-court press on a handful of other clients in hopes of flushing the story about Noah and me out of the news cycle, and the tactic had worked like a charm. It had served us well more times than I could count over the years. I never figured I would have to use it for myself.

Everything had gone back to normal. I had to remind myself of that, and it was becoming something close to a chant in my head. Nothing changed. Everything was the same. I had my business, Noah had his, and our lives were back on track just as they had been before.

If only I could erase the past several weeks, going back to the first night at Club Caramel. There was no going back to living life as I had before now that I knew how much better, brighter, and more exciting it could be.

Settling back in the seat, my arms around myself, I gazed out the window at the endless stretch of clouds under the jet. It was all sunny and bright up here, far above it all.

Was he thinking about me? Wondering what I was doing, how I was handling things? He hadn't called to find out, but then I had shut and locked that door on my own. He had wanted to talk, and I had made that impossible. There was nobody but myself to blame.

The worst part? I couldn't forget him. This wasn't like the average ruined relationship, where both parties could go their merry way and avoid each other. I would never be rid of him. We shared too much history. If Rose and Colton ever got married, I had no doubt Noah would be his best man. We would be thrust together time and again unless I moved across the country or something. Since that wasn't going to happen, I had no choice but to look forward to years of looking at him and seeing our past.

Knowing there was so much more to him than what he showed the world.

Knowing I still wanted him.

The only thing that could make this trip better would be having him next to me. When I imagined myself indulging over four days in the Maldives, there was no excitement— nothing to look forward to but loneliness.

After starting four different movies but stopping out of boredom within the first twenty minutes, I pulled out my phone to scroll through any new emails before sedating myself with social media scrolling. It wasn't easy to turn off my work brain and simply enjoy mindless scrolling, but that was still preferable to questioning every single one of the decisions I made over the past weeks.

I was scrolling through Reddit when a text came through from Rose. Strange, but she hadn't seemed too surprised to find out about her brother and me. Or maybe she didn't want to look like the complete hypocrite my brother was, blowing up my phone, threatening to kick Noah's ass. It was nothing but talk. Rose had probably pointed out how stupid Colton sounded. Either way, even his anger had fizzled before long.

Rose's text came with an attached link.

Rose: *Thought you might want to see this. *smiley face emoji.**

Tapping the link took me to an Instagram account.

Noah's account.

Emotion lodged in my throat in time with my heart clenching. Why would she send me to his Instagram? I had gone out of my way to avoid any specifics when she'd pretty much forced me into confessing whatever we were, but she knew I was confused and full of regret. Why shove him in my face?

It took all of three seconds for me to understand once a video began to play. Taken on his phone, by the looks of it, while he sat in his living room looking painfully gorgeous as always. Longing hit me like a sledgehammer and left me breathless.

"Hi, everybody." His easygoing smile made me smile back. "There's been a lot about me in the press lately, positive and otherwise. Until now, I've relied on others to do the speaking for me, but it's clear there's something I need to straighten out in my own words."

Oh, no. This had the potential to be an absolute disaster.

His shoulders rose and fell before he continued. "I've made a lot of mistakes... more than I could count if I tried. One of them led to a series of false accusations made against me. Without my publicist, Sienna Black, I would've inevitably made things worse by shooting off my mouth. She saved me from myself. Unfortunately, becoming involved with me led to trouble for her. I have to apologize for that, deeply and sincerely."

This was the man who didn't apologize. He'd told me so.

"I'm not perfect," he admitted. "I'll make mistakes after today. All I can do is promise to move forward and do better from now on. I hope very much to make things right with anyone I've hurt."

With a wink, he added, "One person in particular. Thank you for watching."

That was it. Short, sweet, and to the point. And in the end, directed at me. At least I hoped it was. He had gone ahead and apologized in front of essentially the whole world. Already, the video had been shared a few hundred times, and he'd only posted it four hours ago. I fired off a text to Jules, asking if she knew anything about it, before setting my phone down with a shaking hand.

I was flying away from him when all I wanted was to be with him. To ask if he was talking about making things right with me, to tell him how proud I was of him for being so humble. What was I thinking? I pulled up his number, ready to demand he fly out to the Maldives so we could talk in person, but I only got as far as his voicemail. The texts I sent to Rose and my cousins went unanswered too.

I was literally hanging in midair for the rest of the flight.

There was a car waiting for me at the private hangar, leaving me with nothing to do but try Noah repeatedly. The gorgeous slice of paradise all around me went unnoticed while I obsessed over what was supposed to happen next. All the while, Noah's video racked up shares and likes.

When the car's progress slowed, I looked out the window toward the luxury villa looming up ahead. The beachfront villas would be available for purchase once the resort opened, while a series of smaller waterfront cottages would be up for rent by short-term vacationers. I'd be staying in a two-story, three-bedroom villa with a thatched roof and a private garden surrounded by a sparkling pool. In other words, Heaven. My temporary slice of it.

Remember what you're here for.

My emotions were all over the place by the time I stepped out of the car, and I was starting to wonder why everyone in my life had suddenly put me on the Pay No Mind list, but I was here for business. I forced myself to pay attention to my lush surroundings as I walked out onto the white sandy beach, already prepared to recommend the resort to anybody looking for a private paradise. The sapphire water lapped at the sand, begging me to dip my toes in.

"What do you think?"

I jumped, yelping when a deep voice cut through the conflict buzzing in my brain. It didn't make sense. He wasn't supposed to be here. Yet, Noah walked my way, hands in his pockets, his bare feet sinking into the warm sand. "It's pretty fucking phenomenal out here, isn't it?"

When I found my breath, I asked, "What are you doing here? Did you see I've been calling you for hours? Why did you make that video? Were you talking about me?"

He tipped his head to the side. "That sounded like one long word. Try slowing down."

"You are such a dick." A dick whose laughter only set a match to the powder keg that had been ready to explode for hours. My hands closed into fists before I gritted out, "This might be a joke to you, but it's very serious to me. I want answers."

His lids fluttered over brown eyes brimming with confusion. For God's sake, had I genuinely shocked him? Did he know me at all? No, he expected me to melt over a video and a surprise personal appearance. My heart might have been ready to burst with excitement and relief, but I still had a shred of dignity to my name.

"I wasn't trying to piss you off." In a flash, he went contrite, his features pulling together in a pained expression. "I make smart-ass jokes when I'm nervous. In case you hadn't noticed."

"You? Nervous?" I found it difficult to believe. What mattered more just then was watching him squirm under my stare.

"You tell me how I should feel. Standing here like an asshole." He spread his arms out to either side. "Hoping I can make you see how much you mean to me. I was stupid and wrong to push you away that morning at my place. It was a knee-jerk reaction."

"It was a jerk-jerk reaction," I muttered. The fact was, my indignation was melting fast, but I wanted to make him beg a little. It was the least he could do.

"Whatever you want to call it, it was a bad move on my part. I should have stuck by your side the way you stuck by mine."

And now I felt slightly guilty in the face of his contrition. "I did try to walk away after your interview," I reminded him in a softer voice. "But you wouldn't let me get away with it."

"I couldn't let you go." He shrugged, then jammed his hands into the pockets of his linen shorts. "I needed you. I still do. I always will."

The nerve of him saying exactly the right thing at the right time. "Damn you." Sand flew as I marched up to him, taking his striped button-down in my fists and yanking hard. "Damn you for thinking you can follow me out here and win me back with a video." Standing on my tiptoes, I added, "Damn you for being right too."

Understanding barely had the chance to dawn on his handsome face before I crushed my lips to his. His arms shot out and pulled me close, where I belonged.

Adrenaline raced through my system with every rapid, joyful beat of my heart. Who was I kidding? There was no fighting him. Not when my whole world had started revolving around us when I wasn't paying attention. Some-where along the way, I had started needing him. I didn't know how to stop.

By the time the kiss broke and I buried my face in his neck, I was home. I closed my eyes, holding him, letting myself be held against his firm chest. "I'm glad you're here," I decided, smiling when his arms tightened.

"I hope you don't mind everybody ignoring your calls after Rose sent you the link."

"What?" My head snapped up, eyes flying open wide. "You set that up?"

"I figured sending you the video while you were thou-sands of feet in the air would give you time to think about everything." He winced. "Risky, since you could've decided to tell me to fuck myself, but what's life without a little risk?"

"You have a habit of doing that." Letting him go, I folded my arms. "The way you told everybody to pretend they didn't know about your stupid prank. You like to make these arrangements behind my back."

"It was for your sake." He shrugged. "So was this. It's all

for you. I'll do anything to make up for the shit I put you through. Back then and up through today. That's all I want."

My smile was shaky, tearful. The world was in Technicolor again, bright and shining, and all thanks to him. The last man I would ever have expected to fit me like we were made for each other. "I mean, maybe don't take credit for everything," I reminded him because busting his balls was a habit I wouldn't soon grow out of. "The resort is just the perfect backdrop."

"Is it?" He turned partway, craning his neck to admire the sprawling villa. "Did I not tell you I've done business with the owner?"

"You have? Small world." His strange attitude was making me suspicious, to put it mildly.

"You should check out the interior." Turning back to me, grinning, he added, "Since it's yours."

This day was full of surprises. "Pardon?"

"Isn't it what you said you wanted? A house in the Maldives?"

"When did I?" I had said that to him once, hadn't I? Weeks ago. My heart swelled before I whispered, "You remembered that?"

"I do listen sometimes."

"So you set all of this up?"

His head bobbing, he confirmed, "I coordinated with Jules. The fact that the resort is about to open was a coincidence. I can't take credit for that."

This time, when I threw myself into his arms, I wrapped my arms around his neck and kissed him as hard as I could. He had remembered. He bought me a house in paradise and went out of his way to keep it a secret. All to make me happy.

I was weak and breathless by the time I came up for air.

All at once, everything was right again. The world had found out about us and kept turning. I still had my business. His empire was intact. All I needed was to know he was totally with me. I didn't know how to ask for that assurance.

As it turned out, I didn't need to. "I want you to know something." He brushed windswept hair away from my face, his dark eyes gleaming as he stared down at me. The hard, arrogant expression I was accustomed to had softened into something sweet but just as sexy. "You make me want to be a better man. The sort of man you deserve. Somebody who's honest and owns up to his mistakes. You keep me in line and remind me of what's important. Money, business... none of it matters as much as having you. I've been lost without you. Please say we can find a way to make this work because I love you. You're part of me and always will be."

A rush of joy stole every word I ever knew, leaving me sputtering helplessly before he captured my mouth again. This time, our kiss was tender, full of everything neither of us could put into words, sweeping me up into a whirlwind of emotion and sizzling sensation.

"By the way," I told him with a soft laugh between kisses. "I love you too."

He chuckled, nuzzling my neck, holding me close enough that I could feel his heart pounding. "All it took was buying you your dream house, huh?"

"Actually, there are other things I love about you." He looked down at me, quirking an eyebrow, before I ran a hand over his sizable bulge. "Like this, for instance."

He could pretend to be offended all he wanted. I felt the way he jumped against my palm while a wicked grin stirred his lips. "Funny you should mention that since I was about to ask when we could christen every single room in that villa. And there are a lot of them," he pointed out before emitting a deep growl that curled my toes.

"Well, we have four days to cover every square foot." With my arms around his neck, I added, "I guess we better get started."

The next thing I knew, he'd scooped me up in his arms, carrying me across the sand and up to the covered rear porch. Everything came at me in flashes—the gorgeous, warm woods, the abundance of windows and doors to let in the balmy air.

We entered through the kitchen. He couldn't wait more than I could, setting me on the long wooden table and nudging a chair aside to make room for himself between my legs. I hiked up my long, flowing skirt, taking his face in my hands and hungrily pulling him down to kiss him greedily.

Before I left New York, I was sure I would never get to do this again. Now, I had nothing but forever to look forward to.

My heart fluttered with anticipation while he reached between us to free his cock. I closed my legs around his, pulling him in, letting my hands play over his shoulders and back. This was my second chance to touch him, to be touched, to share this thrill with him. I would never take it for granted.

He moved my panties to the side, groaning when he felt how wet he had already made me. "Fuck, I love you," he whispered, impaling me in one quick, deep thrust that made me gasp. We stilled together, holding our breath, eyes locked.

Forever.

Forever with this man.

Yes, I could see that in those endless brown orbs. I could see my future there.

The briefest smile passed over his face as he began to

move. All I could do was wrap my arms around him and hold on tight as he took me on the first of so many more adventures we would experience together. Manhattan, the Maldives, it didn't matter where we were. So long as we were together, we could make our way through anything.

His mouth trailed up my neck before brushing my ear. "In case you were wondering..." he grunted, "... I brought a few special surprises along. It's been too long since I've turned this ass red."

The heat already blazing in my core burst into an inferno.

Forever wouldn't be long enough with him.

EPILOGUE
ARIA

Me: *Sorry, totally forgot about class. I'll be there next time.*

After sending the text to Sienna, I cursed myself for being such a wimp. It was my idea to sign up for Skye's class, but I hadn't had the nerve to show up for two weeks. Not because I couldn't handle it. I loved Skye. She was a freaking genius when it came to motivation.

Working out with her made me feel amazing...

... when there wasn't a weird, strangely aggressive man silently glaring at me the whole time.

I didn't even know if he would be there. I didn't know his name, his age, or anything about him. I didn't know why he seemed to have a problem with me either. He had never said a word. The way he stared and the strange, almost angry energy around him spoke volumes.

That wasn't the worst part. I would've sworn I saw him around outside of class and at Starbucks last week, standing three people behind me in line. I'm also pretty sure I spotted him on the sidewalk outside the restaurant where I had dinner with my sister two nights ago. I told myself to mention him to her to see if she got the same vibe I did. For all I knew, he mistook me for her. She had a habit of leaving devastated men in her wake after dumping them. The girl never cared much about dating the same guy for very long.

But I had chickened out, just like I was skipping out of going to class with Sienna because I got a weird feeling about him.

Instead of going to the spin studio, I headed out to my usual Starbucks to pick up an iced matcha before meeting up with Valentina. If anything, it would be nice to hang out with her for a little bit and forget how squeamish I was about my would-be stalker. I was probably going overboard by thinking of him that way. I even shook my head at myself while waiting for my drink, listening to an audiobook through my AirPods and texting Mom to tell her I was on my way.

"Aria?" I heard the barista call my name, and my head popped up before I stepped closer to the counter, reaching for the cup.

I wasn't fast enough. Somebody snatched it up before I could touch it, somebody tall and muscular with unruly sandy hair. Somebody who smirked down at me while I stared up at him in cold shock. There were no plausible excuses this time. He was definitely following me, and now those icy-blue eyes of his sent dread skittering down my spine.

The sight of his slow, knowing smile didn't do anything to make me feel better. "This yours?" he asked in a deep voice edged with what sounded like an English accent.

"Yes." I held out a trembling hand, curling my fingers inward. "That's mine. Can I have it?"

He lifted a shoulder, extending his arm, pressing the cup

against my open palm. "Sorry for the misunderstanding...
Sis."

My mouth fell open before I pulled out an AirPod with
my free hand. No way had I heard him right. "Excuse me?
What did you just call me?" I asked, ready to laugh.

He wasn't laughing. There wasn't a hint of humor in his
voice when he replied, "I think you heard me, *Sis*. Nice to
finally meet you."

To be continued....

READ ARIA'S STORY NEXT...

Delicious Tropes you can expect:
Stepbrother Trope, Enemies to Lovers, Revenge and Hidden
Desires

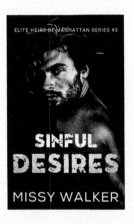

Preorder SINFUL DESIRES today!

BONUS SCENE

Don't want to let Noah and Sienna go just yet?

Grab the FREE bonus scene here:
https://dl.bookfunnel.com/2x99duw6x5

ALSO BY MISSY WALKER

JOIN MISSY'S BOOK BABES

Hear about exclusive book releases, teasers, discounts and book bundles before anyone else.

Sign up to Missy's newsletter here:
www.authormissywalker.com

Become part of Missy's Facebook Reader Group where we chat all things books, releases and of course fun giveaways!

https://www.facebook.com/groups/missywalkersbookbabes

ACKNOWLEDGMENTS

This story poured out of me so quickly, and for that, I'm grateful. Some characters speak to me with ease, while others make me feel like I'm pulling teeth just to get a single word on the page.

A huge thank you to my beta readers and editors, whose insights and support help shape these stories into what they become. Chantell, Kay and Nicki, you are so awesome. My beautiful betas, Ella, Karmin, Maria and Saskia, thank you!!

Thank you to all my fans, especially my facebook reader group Missy Walkers Book Babes! As long as you keep reading my stories, I'll continue delivering billionaire play-boys and characters with rich, complex emotions that will hopefully keep you turning the pages late into the night.

Much love,

Missy x

ABOUT THE AUTHOR

Missy is an Australian author who writes kissing books with equal parts angst and steam. Stories about billionaires, forbidden romance, and second chances roll around in her mind probably more than they ought to.

When she's not writing, she's taking care of her two daughters and doting husband and conjuring up her next saucy plot.

Inspired by the acreage she lives on, Missy regularly distracts herself by visiting her orchard, baking naughty but delicious foods, and socialising with her girl squad.

Then there's her overweight cat—Charlie, chickens, and border collie dog—Benji if she needed another excuse to pass the time.

If you like Missy Walker's books, consider leaving a review and following her here:

instagram.com/missywalkerauthor
facebook.com/AuthorMissyWalker
tiktok.com/@authormissywalker
bookbub.com/profile/missy-walker

Printed in Great Britain
by Amazon